T0166657

PRAISE FOR AIDAN HIGGINS

"This carefully constructed and intelligent book . . . is ironic and witty in its juxtapositions."

—*Saturday Review*

"*Scenes from a Receding Past* is ironic and tender, like *Langrishe, Go Down*, and equally informative about love."

—*New Statesman*

"Higgins is very good at recreating the feeling of release and free flow of all senses that comes with the first bouts of physical love."

—*Guardian*

"Clearly the best Irish novel since *At Swim-Two-Birds* and the novels of Beckett."

—*Irish Times*

OTHER BOOKS BY AIDAN HIGGINS

SCENES FROM
A RECEDING PAST

AIDAN HIGGINS

Dalkey Archive Press

NORMAL · LONDON

First Dalkey Archive edition, 2005

Library of Congress Cataloging-in-Publication Data:

Higgins, Aidan, 1927–
    Scenes from a receding past / by Aidan Higgins. — 1st Dalkey Archive ed.
        p. cm.
    ISBN 1-56478-387-1 (acid-free paper)
    1. Teenage boys—Fiction. 2. Young men—Fiction. 3. Ireland—Fiction.
I. Title

    PR6058.I34S3 2005
    823'.914—dc22
                                            2004063483

Partially funded by a grant from the Illinois Arts Council, a state agency.

Dalkey Archive Press is a nonprofit organization located at Milner Library
(Illinois State University) and distributed in the UK by
Turnaround Publisher Services Ltd. (London).

www.dalkeyarchive.com

CONTENTS

Part I

Part II

This book is for
my sons
Carl Nicolas
Julien John
Elwin James

I

I should like to have heard, as I did, those murmurs made by villages in the morning, in the evening and that other murmur which, together with the memories of childhood, voices make within us when we know that we shall never hear them again, voices of the dead.

Yves Berger—*The Garden*
Translated from the French *Le Sud* by Robert Baldick

I do not long for the world as it was when I was a child. I do not long for the person I was in that world. I do not want to be the person I am now in that world then.

I've been examining half-scraps of my childhood. They are pieces of distant life that have no form or meaning. They are things that just happened like lint.

Richard Brautigan
Revenge of the Lawn

Author's Note

The Sligo Town mentioned here is (or was) Celbridge, Co. Kildare; the River Garavogue therefore the River Liffey; Lissadell House being Killadoon House in the latter county, and Slish Wood—Killadoon Wood. Nullamore was Springfield where I was born. The details given are not always true; those gentle times, those guileless gossoons, are now consigned to oblivion.

'Auckland'—the lawyer's office, Olivia's home—is (or was), King Williams Town in the Eastern Province of South Africa, with an admixture of East London, S.A. (the public baths).

'The most flittering light of old Parma's school' was, in fact, Il Correggio, christened Antonio Allegri and not Paolo Veronese.

The Listener transcript is taken from Alan Benett's 'The Pith of Reality' (May 1976).

CHAPTER I

Distant Figures

I am three years old. Someone guides my hand. The hand writes out 'I am DAИ.'

I am Dan.

The same big hairless hand now holding a dessert spoon brings a spoonful of porridge to my mouth. I have a small mouth, a little swallow. I am hungry, taste warm oatmeal, creamy milk, demerara sugar, it all dissolves inside me. It's winter. The days are often cold. In the mornings the kitchen is cold. Old Mrs Henry is our cook. She looks like a hen.

She looks like Ma Duggy White the speckled hen. When Ma Duggy White drones, Wally says the noise means 'Years-gone-by.' Wally is my brother.

When the woodchips catch fire in the range and the coal catches, flames shoot up the flue. Sometimes the edge of the spoon cuts my lip. My mouth is too small for the dessert spoon. The spoon touches the edge of the plate and then carries it to my mouth. Why is it that it touches the edge of the plate before coming to my mouth?

The porridge plate has a thick edge. On the bottom there is a design. As the porridge disappears the picture emerges. Always the same picture, the same pair. He thin and fleeing, she fat and following with a rolling-pin. Sometimes I am fooled. I am too eager and must wait for the dipping spoon, checked by the big hairless hand. I think then that it must be the wrong picture or the wrong plate, another plate—as the old picture appears, but set at a different angle, upside-down or sideways, the thin and affrighted Jack Spratt chased forever by his fat and furious wife.

The hand that conveys the spoon of porridge to my mouth belongs to Gina Green. Gina (Geena) Green lives in Dromore West. Her granny is still alive, though very old. Gina is not

11

her real name. I cannot say her real name. I call her Geena.

She is my nurse and Wally's. Wally is my elder brother. He is not sweet on Geena Green. I am.

My father holds me in his arms at the window, pointing to the wonders of the world without. A goat in a tree, flying fish over a meadow, sailing boats disappearing into clouds. I fidget in his arms, turning like a top, always missing the sailing boat hidden in clouds, the goat hidden in the leaves, the flying fish hidden in the meadow. All I see are clouds, cowslip in the meadow, a tree quivering.

'Ah Da! Ah Da!' I cry, twisting and turning in his arms. My father holds back his head and laughs. He smells of hair-grease, linseed oil, his quiff is parted in the middle.

'Look!' he says, 'there, Dan. Can you see it?'

'Ah *Da*!'

I draw featureless line-men, with straight lines for their arms and legs, a circle for the face, with broomhandle hair, and vacant expressions on their moon-faces.

I go to sleep with the black cat between my legs. Puss creeps under the sheet, becomes my water-bottle. The room is cold. Wally grinds his teeth in his sleep. The wind from the Atlantic rattles and buffets the windows, the venetian blinds shift and stir. The house is adrift, Nullamore off its moorings, the black cat sleeps in the crook of my arm, its whiskers and its purring tickle my face. It has a tiger's face. The wind moans outside, the Atlantic is tearing itself to bits. I think of sailors lost in it.

'Got any tickles?'

'No.'

'I just don't believe you,' the hearty aunt says. Her insistent fingers dig into me, strong practical hands torture me. 'Got any tickles now? . . . Got any tickles for me?' I

12

tumble off the sofa, squirm like a snake on the carpet, wetting myself. The hearty aunt is all over me, tickling, laughing. I lie on the carpet. An amused strange face watches me. Aunty G. is a famous horse-woman.

By accident I light a match against my teeth. It flares in my mouth.

'Honour thy father and thy mother,' I write.

Two separate layers of dirty white clouds come slowly together over the wood, between them the early September moon hangs, three-quarter full. Alongside the wood, cricketers play in a field, their flannels whiter than the moon, whiter than the dirty clouds, they move like robots, above them the clouds draw slowly together, the moon disappears. 7.15 pm. On September 2, 1930.

What do they want of me, that speechless pearl-grey company, standing huddled together watching me. Are they Mormons? Sometimes in my dreams they appear, wringing their veined hands, looking at me with their afflicted eyes. Behind, immense banks of clouds rear up. Are they dreading a dust-storm? A bunch of dirt farmers with no time to read. Mormons—even the name looks strange. They stand speechless in the depthless pearl-grey of oncoming afternoon, observing me.

I see the legs of a tinker-man sticking out of a barrel in the deserted lane. Tinkers live in empty tar-barrels, then? A fire smoulders on the grass verge, tattered clothes, rags, hang on the bush. A gypsy woman watches me.

'Who wants a piggy-back ride?' my father asks, down on his hands and knees.

I ride on his back. He is an elephant. We are in India. I hold his huge elephant ears, he trumpets, his back shakes. He

13

bucks me off behind the sofa. He is no longer an elephant but a bucking bronco. I am a cowboy.

Time passes in Dromore West. A strong wind from the Atlantic buffets the windows.

The Atlantic is an ocean. Geena Green teaches me the abc. She writes: 'The cat jumped from under the bed and bit me.' I copy this out at her bidding, her hand holding mine.

I write: 'I can swim like a fish in the sea.' And on a fresh page: 'The man was smoking on the beach.'

Geena takes us to Bundoran beach. She does not take off her clothes or go swimming. She cannot swim, walking in an abstracted way by the water's edge. I am afraid of the ocean and its smells. It smells of hugeness and dark tangled seaweed and lostness. The Atlantic is full of drowned men and women, children too. I watch Geena, feeling solicitude. (It's an expression used often by my mother—'all solicitude').

I watch Geena Green walking on Bundoran sands. She is big and strong. But the ocean is immense. The air itself is as strong as the smelling salts that my mother keeps by her bed in a dark green bottle capped with a glass stopper.

Lizzy Bolger puts on face powder and red lipstick and kisses me on the cheek. She has a funny smell. Geena has a nice smell. My mother always has a nice smell.

My ears are frozen, my eyes water, I am holding Geena Green's hand, I do her bidding. My legs are raw where the shorts chaff them. The wind goes through me. Before getting into bed I kneel and pray: 'AngelofGod myGuardiandear towhomGod'slovecommitsmehere everthisdaybeatmyside tothisandthat toruleandguide Amen.' Geena says 'Amen' and tucks me in, saying: 'And now sleep well.' I hear the great Atlantic roaring and tearing at the coast and Wally snoring in the next bed. Then it's morning once more. Nine blackbirds fly around the room.

I wrote: 'Wunc there were two men cold laurel and hardy

14

they were cworelling all day.' And: 'There was this ophill creature he could eat people.' I write: 'Joudy gets the beyby then she says *you* get the beyby now *you* get the beyby im going to get the soseges thoump were *is* the beyby daun sters the sosegis i get the soseges goup *you* give the so igis to me goup.'

'Very imaginative,' Geena Green says.

Her mother is a tall serious woman with a long face who stands with folded arms in the doorway of their cottage and keeps her eyes on the comings and goings in the street. Geena Green's grandmother is a little crabby woman with a lined face. The dark corridor is full of bicycles. They all live in the kitchen, a dark room. I write to Geena: 'Gives a ckis no gives ackis no gives a ckis.' I do not show it to her but hide it under my pillow. Geena tells me that I am making good progress.

I write: 'In the at lantik ochen ther was a mermade . . .' Geena looks over my shoulder, smiling. 'Yes,' she says, 'and then what happened?'

I write: . . . 'one day there came a storm and the mermaid was swept to chore where there lived a king who was the sun of the gods and there was this lovely queen one day they had a baiby.'

Our car is a Coatelen-Hillman with spoke wheels and solid tyres. My brother Wally is a good boy. He does what he is told. He is two years older than I. I do not do what I am told. I wet the bed. I write with squiggley letters: 'They decide to steal Princess Philadelphia and split half the money between them. They put kloroform on Princess Philadelphia and King Edward finds out saying 3, ooooooooooo rupies.'

It's evening. I'm hungry. I do not like Dublin that distant city. The green bus leaves from the quays. The river stinks. I feel sick. My hair, cut at Maison Prost and set with stiffener, holds the crown of my head in a vice. I get sick on the bus. I love Sligo and never want to leave home. I love my mother and my father and old Mrs Henry and the Bowsy Murray, though not always.

I write with a sharpened pencil in flowery lettering: 'Some

of the Romans in Pompeii started poking spears into the lava balls.' I write: 'The giant heard the boy laughing in the mountains.' And on a fresh page: 'The sun comes up with colours and the man wakes up.'

Wally makes water-colour pictures of sand-coloured lions and orange-and-black-striped tigers jumping with outstretched claws towards little hunters in khaki, pith helmets, puttees, their claws and sometimes their heads disappear into the puff of smoke from the rifle. In a jungle full of creepers and snakes wreathing about immensely tall trees, the same drama recurs, but now the savage beasts have shorter space to spring from, the little brown-faced hunters kill them coolly.

'The giant had a tiny hand and he passed me,' I write carefully in pencil. The pencil sharpener is a little globe of the world. I put the head of the pencil in and turn the globe, and the blue-and-white globe revolves in my hand and pencil shavings curl out. I like the smell of lead and new pencils.

'Spelling improving,' Geena Green says.

We eat fish on Fridays. We are Catholics. The Protestants do not eat fish on Friday or attend Mass on Sunday. They have a different church, a different bell, and they look different to Catholics. The Bowsy Murray blesses himself before he eats. He says the Angelus. Old Mrs Henry and Lizzy Bolger say the rosary in the kitchen. Lizzy Bolger is our maid. Bowsy Murray and old Mrs Henry and Lizzy are Catholics. We live in Sligo, but I was born in Dromore West.

Sligo is a grey town and a fast river flows through it, the river Garavogue. We go on holiday to Mulranny and Bundoran. I write:

    'Dan Ruttle,
    Nullamore,
    Sligo.
    Ireland.'

I write: 'Se se se se se sede se pe se ar se Le, pe, ke, pe, le, he, se, de, se, be . . .'

'But what does it mean?'Geena Green asks.

'I don't know. It's writing.'

'But it must mean *something*, sillybilly.'

'It does mean something.'

'What?'

'I don't know.'

'Well then . . .'

Now I no longer love Geena Green. She does not understand me. Perhaps she has never understood me. Now I love the Bowsy Murray and Lizzy Bolger and my mother, but not Geena Green.

My mother kisses me good-night. 'Too old to cry,' she whispers. High over Nullamore I hear the wet cry of a curlew. The great beech tree makes its deep persistent groan, grinding down all its length. My mother says in a sing-song voice:

Hush-a-bye, baby, on the tree top,

When the wind blows the cradle will rock;

When the bough breaks the cradle will fall,

Down will come baby, cradle and all.

'Sleep tight,' she says, going out the door. Now there is only the night-light and Wally grinding his teeth.

The Bowsy Murray wears a butcher's apron tied behind, stained with blood, it reaches to his ankles. He wears leather gaiters over boots with ironbound toecaps that turn up. He sits in the kitchen—a tubby little man stirring the tea which old Mrs Henry has poured out for him. She puts milk and sugar into the mug first. He drains this into a saucer, lowering his head to slurp it up like a dog drinking. Then he wipes his drooping walrus moustache with one finger and brings out a curly pipe. His fingers are stained with tobacco and blood. He pares off some shag with his weathered knife.

The Bowsy works for Young the butcher as slaughterer and delivery-boy, and brings us our Sunday roast regularly every Saturday. He served in the British Army.

17

'The Bowsy stinks,' Wally says.

'You must never say that of a poor working man,' Geena Green says.

For lost things, my mother advises a prayer to St. Anthony, and the lost things turn up again in odd places: the half-solid ball behind the hotpress door, the yo-yo in the knitting basket, the bat under the bath.

I know it. I know it now.

> One-two, buckle my shoe;
> Three-four, knock at the door;
> Five-six, pick up sticks.
> Seven-eight, lay them straight;
> Nine-ten, a big fat hen . . .

I can repeat it. I know it all.

On the verge of sleep, I hear an intruder climb the paling below, jump heavily onto the gravel, heavy footsteps drag slowly across the gravel, up the steps, through the open front door. Crossing the hall, the dragging footsteps begin to ascend the stairs, they approach across the landing, halt before the nursery door, which remains open. Rigid with fright I sink slowly down under the bedclothes, but not soon enough. The horror has already entered, the huge shadow crowds across the ceiling, lit by a lurid blue light from Geena Green's altar. The apparition fills the bedroom—army boots and puttees, pith helmet, a heavy service revolver in its holster, a baggy cavalry uniform, all worn like a scarecrow.

I hear the glass case being opened. The intruder does what he has come to do. In his own good time he leaves, making no attempt at secrecy. The footsteps retreat down the landing, down the stairs, onto the gravel, over the paling, across the meadow, into the plantation. I come out from under the bedclothes. Wally's bed is empty. The glass case hangs open. The shelves are empty, the toys and books gone, a note in a criminal hand is stuck to the glass.

Presently, I hear water running in the bathroom, then water flushing in the lav. Wally comes in with his hair sleeked back. He removes his dressing gown with elaborate ceremony, says his prayers, climbs into bed. As soon as his head touched the pillow he rises straight up. Standing on his bed for maximum effect he points dramatically at the empty shelves, the note.

'Hey, what's going on here?'

I know it's Wally up to his tricks, but I cannot accuse him. It was Wally dressed up in Uncle Edmund's uniform, trying (succeeding) to put the wind up me. But the monstrous boots had seen action, the pith helmet too, the service revolver, all these gave the lie to the known and the familiar. False Walter moved as if in a trance, his actions mannered, portentious, doors opened at one touch. I could no more confront that than I could jump out the window. Wally had moved as if hypnotised, weighed down with dark power.

'Brave little Belgium,' my mother says. The rain falls vertically, scouring deep holes in the gravel before Nulla-more. I stare down at the pitted gravel, the tea-coloured water. Rabbits come out of the plantation, a pheasant, when the rain blows over, the grass glistens. I hear the choked-off call of the pheasant. I study sepia snaps of Jus Moorkens standing with folded arms outside a dugout on the Western Front. He wears a curious ridged helmet; he waits for the gas attack with Belgian troops. A troop train travels towards the front, its carriages marked 'Hommes-Chevaux.' Behind him, shellholes filled with water, broken trees, a low miserable sky full of rain. My mother, seated in the window embrasure, knits a pullover, pulling out wool.

Nurse O'Reilly backs horses, gives us the used betting stubs marked with a thick red and blue pencil. Wally and I sit in the pram, too old for prams, outside the bookie's office. The pram begins to move, gathering speed on the pavement slope. Wally cries out. Nurse O'Reilly comes running. The pram

careers down the slope, Wally bawling, I rigid with fear. A
roadmender in hobnail boots stops the runaway pram.
Nurse O'Reilly is white in the face.

In the nursery Nurse O'Reilly recites:

There was a little man, and he had a little gun,
And his bullets were made of lead, lead, lead;
He went to the brook, and shot a little duck
Right through the middle of the head, head, head.

In the kitchen Lizzy Bolger recites:

There was a little man, and he had a little gun,
Up to the mountains he did run,
With a belly-full of fat and an old Tom cat.
And a pancake stuck to his bum, bum, bum.

In the study Wally and I recite this to our father.

'That's not nice,' he says.

Nurse O'Reilly recites:

He carried it home to his old wife Joan,
And bade her a fire for to make, make, make,
To roast the little duck he had shot in the brook,
And he'd go and fetch her the drake, drake, drake.

Wally invents names for everything. One face I wear he
calls 'The Bear's Face' (in the cold, frozen in shorts,
miserable, squinting into the lens of the Box Brownie),
another is 'The Guilty Look'.

'Stinky, stinky, parley voo,' Wally says.

'Mafeking is relieved!' he shouts.

Wielding cricket stumps for broad-swords, with cricket
pads strapped onto our arms as bucklers, we clank in heavy
armour into a clearing in the plantation to fight a duel of
honour. A girl with long blonde hair waits weeping for the
outcome, locked away in a high tower. The bamboos rustle,
the dinner bell is rung at the door of the yard, Wally, groin
impaled against a tree, cries 'Pax!'

The gramophone plays, dust rises, the heavy records
revolve, music smelling of old herbs issues from the slatted
side of the gramophone-box, a reedy male voice sings:

20

As you walk along the Bois de Boulogne
You can hear the girls declare
He must be a millionaire, he must be a millionaire!
I try to imagine Europe. Jus Moorkens outside his dugout waiting for the gas-attack; the trains marked 'Hommes-Chevaux.' A beery voice sings in German—the music of Franz Lehar. I try to imagine Vienna. People are dancing. A carriage draws up before a lighted ballroom. Richard Tauber in a high, high voice sings 'Girls were made to love and kiss.' Georges Gautier, singing in English, enters the chorus of 'O Bella Marguerita!' like a car running down-hill without breaks. 'Picking grapes with you,' he sings with much ardour.

Then, 'The Stein Song', and 'Hold Your Hand Out, You Naughty Boy', 'The Man Who Broke the Bank of Monte Carlo', and 'Betty Co-Ed'. The voices are jolly; high, strange male voices. Music makes me feel sad.

Wally comes clanking towards me, cricket pads now worn as breast-plates, enamel chamber-pot strapped to his head. 'No surrender!' Wally cries in a choked voice. 'I'll make mincemeat of thee, varlet!' Our stump-swords meet with a ring of steel.

A ship, under full sail, with flags flying from the mizzen, waits in the bay. Errol Fynn, smiling gallantly, leaps onto a rock, leaving Basil Rathbone dead in a pool. Ronald Colman fights Douglas Fairbanks. I wade downstream, the wind blows in my long hair, I feel the weight of my sword. Wally is cutting quarter-staves in the plantation. I hear black slaves singing. A horn sounds in a forest.

I press down on my 2B pencil, the lead breaks. A trap-door opens. A harsh voice says, 'Villain!'

'On guard!' I cry in a thin voice.

A little boy is flung from high battlemented walls. Rome burns. My father pokes into his ear with the end of a match.

'What's going on here?'

'Nothing,' I say, looking innocent.

'Be careful with those stumps. You could put out your brother's eye.'

Wearing a loose woollen jersey of candy stripes, the stitching gone here and there, and Wellington boots with the tops turned down, Wally fighting with a bamboo sword falls backwards into the clump of bamboos, both hands clapped to his right eye. He opens his hand, shows me his pierced eyeball gushing blood. 'Pax!'

My mother, by chance, meets her idol Noël Coward in the Shelbourne in Dublin. *'It's Noël!'* she tells my father. Noël Coward, suave as can be, sits with crossed legs, smoking a cigarette in a long holder, conversing in low tones with a beautiful young man.

'Will you not introduce me?' my mother says, carried away by the occasion.

'My secretary.'

England. The Queen-Mother and the little Princesses waving from a balcony; a stuffy voice on the radio saying 'We and our Sister States in the Commonwealth' (I imagine a white man stewing in a pot whom stark naked savages are awaiting to devour). Soho lies underground. Race-gangs knock the points off the railings and file them down to dagger sharpness. In the Gorbels the Scots gangsters have razor blades in the peaks of their caps; small, taciturn men, dangerous.

CHAPTER II

The Banners of Passion Week

The banners of Passion Week, embroidered like battle standards, glisten in purple and violent emerald above the pews in the Cathedral. The officiating priest sings in a phenomenally high voice 'Credo in unum Deum.' The mixed choir responds in a deep collective drone. Incense ascends to the roof. I taste metal in my mouth. I read IHS, IHS, IHS on the banners, I see the nails, the crown of thorns. For Passion Week the statues are shrouded in purple. The incense and deep chanting makes me dizzy. 'Descant singing,' my mother says, 'heavenly.' I try to think of Heaven. The old priest moves in a dream, his heavy vestments held by two serving priests. Flowers from Nullamore garden decorate the High Altar where hundreds of candles burn. A heavy shower begins to pelt the roof outside, blown in from the Atlantic. I read my prayer book, feeling holy.

I have done it in my trousers again. I take short mincing steps, wishing I were somewhere else, someone else, perhaps walking in China, wishing I were dead. The hours pass. The long day drags on. The smell lessens. It hardens. I sit. I hope no one notices, avoiding my father's long nose.

'Funny smell in here,' my father says, breezing into the study where I am reading. 'Smells stuffy in here. I'll just throw open the window.'

'You'll do no such thing,' my mother says. 'It's freezing outside.'

'It's . . .' my father says, and stops, sniffing.

They both look at me.

'Oho,' my father says, holding his nose.

'Have you done it in your trousers by any chance?'

'No.'

23

'Have a look anyway,' my father says.

'Come,' my mother says.

'No.'

'Oh?' my father says. 'That's no way to talk to your mother.'

'No need to,' I say, rigid with shame.

My mother stands behind me, unloosens my braces, opens my shorts.

'Oh dear,' my mother says. 'He's done it in his trousers again.'

My father leaves the room with a rolled newspaper under one arm, whistling.

I stand on the bathroom mat as my mother runs hot water. 'It isn't much,' she says. She cleans and powders me, fetches clean shorts from the hot-press. The trousers smell strange, new lining and clean tweed. They smell like Herbie Lynch.

'Be sure and go in time,' my mother says. 'Ask Gina to help you.'

I think: No fear.

'Yes, Ma,' I say.

'Finiculi Finicula!' I say.

Tommy Flynn claps me on the shoulder.

'Me own!' he says. He takes his accordian down from the nail in the harness-shed, moves one boot on a chair, moves his head to one side and draws out the accordian.

Nurse fishes it out. I lean forward. She holds me by the braces. I make pooley. Wally stands over it. 'Nop much,' he says. I hate his fat legs, his fat cheeks, his positive ways.

Nurse O'Reilly has buck teeth. She comes from Cavan. She nursed my mother when Wally was born. She stands with Uncle Jack, both of them belting fags beside the caravan. Wally and I, dressed in sailor suits, with hands behind our backs, watch Maeve and Honor Healy pulling faces at the camera. The photo appears in the heavy album,

24

Nurse O'Reilly squinting at the camera with a cigarette in her mouth, Uncle Jack with one foot on the caravan step, Aunty Norah looking out the caravan door.

'Press,' Nurse says.

'There's nothing there,' Wally says, pressing.

'Well, press harder, numbskull.'

Wally turns red about the gills. I hear a plop in the water. An unpleasant stink rises.

'That's better,' Nurse says. 'Good boy.'

Wally stands looking complacently out the window of the lav while nurse wipes him and buttons him up.

'Now, Mister-me-lad,' Nurse says to me.

I mount the rostrum with my shorts down. I watch a stray brown dog going into the bleach-green. It cocks its legs against the bamboos. The grass is frozen stiff. I see steam rise.

'Nothing,' I say.

'Goose,' Nurse says, 'Just try.'

Wally stands at the door in a short overcoat, well muffled up, wearing Wellington boots.

'Everything honkey-dorey?' Wally asks.

I push off from the ash-pit, pedal very slowly through the yard gateway, my father's hand on the small of my back, his encouraging words in my ear. He lets go, giving me a push, I cannot turn onto the back avenue, the front wheel begins to wobble, I pedal into a bush.

Wally leaves with a creel over his shoulder, off fishing with Tommy Flynn.

In the study I read bound copies of Strand Magazine. The son goes into his father's study. He stands with his hands behind his back. He says: 'Honestly, Sir, I'd feel better after a good thrashing.' He has a fever in the night. His older sister brings him a glass of water. He is delirious. I study the illustration of the son facing the father, who is seated behind a desk.

25

Plum puddings hang from hooks on the kitchen ceiling.
Lizzy Bolger sings:
            . . . when stors come out to play,
            South of the border, down Mexico way.
I watch her painted lips saying 'stors'.

Wally writes along the kitchen wall in an exquisite hand:
            At the edge of All the Ages
            A Knight sate on his steed . . .

Magic words: Avignon, Babylon, Alabama.

I write: 'The great garden was very beautiful but the robbers
took everything away. After they past the bugs stung them
and they fell to the ground.'
    I copy what my mother writes: 'Ou puis-je changer de
l'argent? Veuillez me reveiller a l'heure.'
    'Ou,' my mother says, correcting it with her pen. 'Not *our*.
What does it mean, Dan?'
    I do not know. It's in French.
    My mother's fountain-pen has a broad nib. I refill it, with
finger and thumb squeeze the little orange sac. My mother's
hand-writing is nice. The cross-strokes are broad like gates.
She speaks sometimes of France, of Parthenay near Poitiers.
The Great War raged. A Zeppelin marked with a German
cross appeared out of the north-east sky, something dark and
cumbersome fell from it; a man in a greatcoat, ballast, a
bomb? A troop train went through Parthenay without
stopping, the carriages marked, 'Homme-Chevaux'. Jus
Moorkens, who had married one of my mother's six sisters,
had volunteered for the Front, but came back gassed.
    ' "Poor little Belgium!" ' my mother said. 'You remember
Jus?'
    Jus Moorkens, gas or no gas, smoked black cigarettes,
spoke in Flemish to Fatty who sat on our caved-in sofa. Wally
and I had to leave the room when we heard them speak in

26

Flemish. They seemed to be gargling.

I write: 'Distant Figures.'

And: 'I was at home i so some little people far a way i told my mother that we shud go doun ther and have a look wen we went ther they were huge so we told them wot we so and *he* came and had a look he dident anderstand it either so we all got mixed up about it the golf man, mayour, king, a dwarf he sed because they are very far away so we oll newit.'

'So we all knew it' my mother repeats, marvelling.

A two-pint milk jug smashes on the flagstones of the kitchen, splattering the Bowsy's polished black gaiters. He leaves immediately by the side door, collecting his basket, cramming on his cap.

In a fit of rage I have overturned the heavy kitchen table.

'Yule cotch it hot, young fella-me-lad, when yewer Doddy hurs of duss, I'm telling yew,' old Mrs Henry says, down on her knees with a rag.

Old Mrs Henry and Lizzy and old Mrs Henry's son set the long table on its legs again.

'That rotten temper of yours will get you into trouble one day,' my mother says.

'I don't care.'

'You may, Sonny Jim, when your dear father comes home and hears of this,' my mother says in a thin voice.

I hide behind the mangle where the cats make their stinks.

'Let him stay there and cool off.'

I smell dirty mangle water, cat-stench, the rollers exude black grease. I want to run away from home. I do not love my mother any more, nor old Mrs Henry, and Lizzy is deceitful. Then I hear the klaxon sounding at the gate, and presently the sound of the returning car. My father is home from golf. But they keep silent before him and I am not punished. I escape into the plantation.

'No supper for yew, me lad,' Lizzy says spitefully.

'Don't care.'

27

At Christmas, at the back of the Cathedral by the confessional, in the crib among the straw, the Holy Family look dead. Joseph crouches, staring with a dead man's eyes at the dead mannikin in the straw. A coffin waits at the back, mounted on trestles. My father stands at the corner of the garden, with his hands behind his back, looking up at the sky.

'The days are drawing out,' he announces.

A coal-fire burns in the grate. Old Mrs Henry is roasting a rabbit in the oven. I like roast rabbit with bread stuffing. I eat meals back to front, working from trifle back to soup. I see a rabbit hung in the larder with dried blood on its nose. A bluebottle buzzes against the window-screen. The larder is cold. With a very red face Lizzy Bolger works the churn in the dairy. I write on one wall of the kitchen: 'The fat cowboy breaks stones in the mountains.' And then, in chalk behind the door: 'The cowboy was shot and they put him in the grave.' Rita Phelan sings 'Poor Little Angeline'.

Old Mrs Henry cuts soda bread for me, spreads black currant jam on it. Old Mrs Henry is my best friend. She has a mole on her right cheek with a hair sticking out of it. She talks in a funny way because she comes from Omagh. Omagh is in the north. The Bowsy Murray is the fat cowboy breaking stones in the mountains. Sweat runs off him. He stinks as usual, fresh sweat, old dried blood, leather, shag tobacco—the smell of an old man. He wears a broad leather belt with studs. His life is not easy. He kills and cuts up cows and pigs, delivers the orders after Young the butcher has prepared them. The Bowsy cycles miles in all weathers on his stiff delivery bike. He comes in black oilskins in winter, wearing a tam o'shanter like Skipper the herring captain.

'The Bowsy Murray is no fool,' my father says. 'Who's drawing all over this wall?'

My father puts his best suit in the oven. The sick black kitten creeps in, the oven door is closed. The kitten is taken out in the morning, stiff as a board. I weep for the passing of the little black kitten.

Out for a drive we run over a cat. I look back, see its guts stuck to the road. Someone has chalked 'UP DEV' and from ditch to ditch another hand has scrawled 'O'DUFFY IS YOUR MAN!'

'Don't look back,' my father says, his gloved hands on the wheel.

Rogation Days mean heat and offerings. The heat of the sun and the closeness of the day sickens me. I walk through meadows, my sandals covered in pollen. I hate my skinny feet, I hate the shape of the sandals.

'The days are drawing out' my father says.

I watch the car going down the front drive. A courting couple are disappearing into the plantation.

'Can you do pooley?' Lizzy Bolger asks.

CHAPTER III

The Bogey Man, the Tantalising Cat and the Nun from Dingle

At a table near the long window in the dining room of the Great Southern Hotel at Bundoran I see the last person in the world I ever want to see. Sitting with his keeper, the Bogey Man is eating prunes. His shoulders are hunched up, spooning prune juice into himself, and I cannot see his face clearly, which may be just as well.

This awful dark figure squats against the light that comes through the long window and falls on the linen tablecloth amid the glassware and silver, and the sight of him puts the fear of God into me. Normally he lives in the cellar at Nullamore with the arrow heads and the empty wine bottles and spider webs, emerging only to properly put the wind up disobedient little brats like me. The keeper watches him moving his heavy shoulders, spooning prune juice; I look for a chain connecting him to table-leg or keeper.

The four of us go to our places.

My mother swims in the sea in a pale blue and white striped costume that opens at the back almost to her dark blue trunks. It confuses me to see my mother in a bathing costume that lays bare so much of her pale skin. Wearing a kimono and tennis shoes she goes out each morning for an early dip.

Sometimes my parents breakfast in the open. My father wears a red scarf inside the collar of his tennis shirt and white shoes with pointed black toe-caps. After breakfast he plays in fourballs with his cronies: Cecil West and Ken Weir and Barney Parr. My mother sometimes joins in foursomes. Golf, in her opinion, is a silly game, merely an excuse for drinking. My father likes to have a ball of malt in the bar after a round. There he is joined by non-playing drinkers: Art Murrable and Willy Prendergast

I write: 'A man saw another man drowning.'

Little grains of sand fall into the stream that flows into the Atlantic. Wearing Wellington boots and sou'westers Wally and I go out with buckets and spades. The Atlantic roars in, collapses, spreads itself out in a pouring over the fine sand and filling the pools. Filling me too with an immense uneasiness. I feel cold. My father is drinking whiskey in the hotel bar. Geena Green collects mussels on the breakwater. I crouch behind a sand dune. Wally has dug a deep hole. I see the last person I want to see, walking along the strand and making in our direction. I feel the pull sucking at my feet. My heart flies into my throat. I hear my mother say that I am a bad boy, that she has a good mind to set the Bogey Man on me.

The Bogey Man is coming for me. From afar he has spotted me. The wind is blowing off the Atlantic, whipping the tails of his greatcoat, he wears a black hat which he holds down with one hand. I watch in horror as he comes for me across the sand. Nothing will ever equal the terror I feel, unable to cry out or run away. The Bogey Man kills by rushing up to his speechless victim and ripping the heart right out of the chest. I sink into the sand as he approaches.

The Bogey Man has arrived at the stream. I see ferocious eyes glaring at me from under the brim of the tall hat. Without breaking his stride he jumps the stream. He makes as if to stop, glaring down at me, but then continues on, holding onto his hat. I watch him go out of sight, becoming smaller and smaller in the distance. Little grains of sand collapse into the stream and are whirled away. My heart begins to beat again.

'Hey!' I hear Wally say. He is holding up a crab. Geena Green picks her way across the channels.

My parents take us on holiday to Bundoran and Mulranny. Looking through a book of pictures I come upon the Bogey Man again, sitting with a round-faced woman who is dressed in a travelling costume and bonnet, sitting close to the Bogey Man who is dressed in brown; his terrible eyes glare out at me. With rugs on their knees they sit in the stern of a departing ship. I read: 'The Last of England'.

I ask Geena Green to come with me into the cellar. I find it empty. The Bogey Man has taken himself off with his woman. Through a magnifying glass I study their faces. I think perhaps they are brother and sister.

I see a cat with a mouse in its mouth. The cat takes it into a corner and plays with it. Tired of playing, curving its paw, pushing, it bites the little head off, begins to eat it. I hear the crunch of small bones.

'Did you ever see a crow flying and a cat sitting on its tail?' my father asks.

'No.' It's a riddle.

'Well, I'll show you,' my father says.

On a blank page of my sketch-book he draws a crow in flight, at least it is a black bird that he calls Crow, turns over a page and draws an obvious cat, all whiskers, sitting on its own tail.

My father shows me the flying crow and the squatting cat. 'There,' he says, laughing, 'look there.' It's a trick question.

I am sick.

If I take the medicines and stay in bed, do as the doctor says, my father promises to give me a surprise present.

'What is it?'

'It's a surprise,' my father says, 'I can't tell you what it is.'

'Tell me what it's *like*,' I say.

My father thinks. It's something with whiskers that you keep in a glass cage. I cannot imagine what this may be. Well again, I forget to ask my father. He too forgets.

Using the end of a match and a nail-file, Wally models Robinson Crusoe in plasticine. A little white-bearded mannikin with a face burnt the colour of terracotta by the implacable island sun, with a hairy hat on his head, a parrot on one shoulder, a fowling-piece resting on his knee, sits under a parasol. Crusoe is like Wally, with his fourteen cats. They breed and run wild, multiply themselves until there are fifty and more running wild about the place, and have to be shot like hares.

Wally is Crusoe all over again, with his close and secretive nature, his habit of hoarding things. He collects Rollos in a cigarette tin and buries it in the lawn.

My uncle is Aubrey Orr, who lives in Dublin in digs with Brinsley MacNamara, poet and novelist, who wrote:

Her shoulders shone
As though polished by the admiration
Of a thousand eyes . . .

My father writes in the same album of poems and beautiful thoughts:

Give thy thoughts no tongue,
Nor any unproportion'd thought his act.
Be thou familiar, but by no means vulgar.
Those friends thou hast, and their adoption tried,
Grapple them to thy soul with hoops of steel.

His married hand-writing is much the same as his hand at Agricultural College.

Aubrey Orr wants to be a detective: he wears rubber soles and follows unsuspecting people about the streets of Dublin. My mother's friend is the writer Crosby Garsten. She knows Percy French. She reads 'Mrs Wiggs of the Cabbage Patch' from the Evening Herald and a serial about a gossiping woman known as Mrs-Win-the-War. I brush and comb my mother's hair. Long brown hairs come out in the comb's teeth. Wally sits in his mother's lap. My mother reads aloud to us: 'Wanted: a detective, to arrest the course of time.'

Summer evenings seem endless. I do not know what to do with myself. My filled sketchbooks depress me. My father comes in with a rug under his arm, back from sunbathing.

'The days are drawing out,' he announces.

I creep down to the kitchen.

'Yewer Ma's run off with a soldjer!' Rita Phelan says

spitefully. She is Lizzy's best friend. Lizzy stands shaking her head at the wash-tub.

'Cry-babbie! Cry-babbie!' Rita Phelan mocks me.

'Don't be at him,' Lizzy says.

The desks are scored with marks from pencils and penknives, we dip our penny pens in the ink. The ink has a queer smell. A big bottle is kept in the closet. Loaded with ink my nib follows the stippled line.

The nun has a red face. She comes from Dingle and has a rough temper to go with the red face. When in a good humour she tells us stories of her youth in West Cork. She sucks lozenges to keep her breath sweet. Her temper is none too sweet.

The strap is kept in a shallow drawer of her desk, the desk itself mounted on a wooden rostrum raised four inches from the floor. Sister Rumold stands when we do not know our times-tables, Catechism or Irish and reaching out she pulls our ears.

She drags at Colfer's ears as though she intended to wrench them off.

'Will I get the strap out? Will I now? Will I now?' her dander and her high colour rising.

The angry nun stands behind Colfer and drags at his ears. Colfer's face is a curious colour.

'Ah be Janey,' Ned Colfer groans, his face close to the scratched and knife-marked desk. 'Ah be Janey!'

'Oh you great numbskull you, Colfer, open those big waxy ears of yours!' the nun cries, leaning over the desk with the strap in her hand. She puts it away again, keeping her eyes on the penny Catechism.

On cold days we sit around the turf fire. The big girls help. Sister Rumold's pets get the ink for her, fill the inkwells. Molly Cushen is one of her pets.

The nun tells us how Michael Collins walked into Dublin Castle with a briefcase marked OHMS under his arm.

Collins is a Martyr of the Rebellion.

A basin of blood stands in the girls' cloakroom. Those who have had teeth pulled are going home early. I watch Molly Cushen who is deadly pale, her face framed by coal-black hair. She holds a bloodsoaked handkerchief to her mouth and her eyes, like sloe-berries, look over the river as a breeze blows hair over her face. She has a strange slurred voice, deep for a girl. She walks slowly over the bridge. The wind blows in her face. I smell the river.

Through my childhood and youth this river runs, spanned by an old stone bridge. The river goes under the old stone bridge. It flows on through this town where I am reared and schooled, first mentioned in the history books when plundered by the Men of the Creeks, the worshippers of Odin who came ashore from their longboats in the first decade of the ninth century. There stands the ruins of the old fort, a fording place in the ancient times long before the telephone and the car; here I grew up.

An old reality, a recurring dream. An old stone bridge, low grey houses of Sligo town, open-window town, the most important in the north-west. Old pipe-smoking men wait on the bridge and spit tobacco juice into the Garavogue. They lean on the bollards down on the quays. I see an acid-faced man sketching there. Jack Yeats, son of John Butler who went over to America and never returned. Brother of WB.

'Now Dan Ruttle, can you say your lesson today?' the nun asks.

Being poor at Irish, I am not one of her pets. I feel her standing close to me, her patience uncertain, sucking a spearmint. Two desks in front, Colfer holds his hands under his arms. The whole row is getting the strap. The nun has taken the strap twice to Colfer. His ears are blazing red where the nun has pulled them.

The days pass. I walk to school. Each day I buy a 2d. Granny Smith. The big girls come screaming like snipe into the Ursuline yard. I jump from behind an archway and take hold of a fistful of hair and haul away. The girl yells into my face. I smell her. Her excitement infects me. I run away. The big girls go running up the ramp.

I am on the Mall. A breeze blows from the Garavogue that drains into Lough Gill. One of my aunts lives on the Mall. She has a sleepy voice and wears heavy skirts that give off a biscuity odour. My aunt offers me Mackintosh's toffees from a big tin. Siphoned lemonade gets into my nose.

'The Countess of Upper Ossary!' my mother says.

I cycle on through the town that's grey like a dream. Coming in on the Markiewicz Road I float through Wine Street into Adelaide Street, then by John Street and Charles Street into Temple, and so by Pond Street and Chapel Street into the Mall again, hearing bells chime in the Cathedral. The old man is sitting on the bollard in the Mall. It's spring.

My head is full of chiming bells as I float on through this little plundered town, avoiding Union Place and Wolf Tone Street because the hard boys like to congregate in those places, waiting to peg stones.

A barrage of stones fall to one side of me.

'Doon an durris mawsh aye doh hulla,' Sister Rumold says.

Moving like an automaton I close the door.

'Uskle an fwinnoge!'

I close the window.

'Cunnus taw tu?'

'Taw may guh mah,' I answer.

'You may sit down now,' Sister Rumold says quietly. The girls are afraid to whisper. The storm has blown over. The strap lies hidden again in the shallow drawer of the desk. I count the minutes and hours until I will be free.

'Ned Colfer, you have me heart-scalded,' Sister says.

She coaxes Colfer. 'You great lug.'

'Gradigy suss, a hain-a-dough! Gradigy suss, gradigy suss,

36

a hain-a-dough!' Sister Rumold says, clapping her hands softly together as we stamp around the classroom, raising dust, repeating 'A hain-a-dough!' An aquatint of a large forlorn dog sitting on a quayside regards us. Colfer is coughing. I smell jammy breath on my neck.

'Gradigy, gradigy, gradigy!' intones Sister Rumold.

She stands beside the open door of the classroom, beating time with her hands, looking amiable, having told us that we are without exception the laziest class she has ever encountered, and that she would prefer to be doing something useful like digging drains or tarring roads, for she is surely wasting her time trying to teach us. I try to imagine Sister Rumold with her skirts furled tarring a road, raising a pick-axe in a drain.

Breaking ranks and cheering the class runs towards the gate. Overhead huge white clouds are piled up, vasty citadels, white castles loom.

CHAPTER IV

My Name, Imaginary Clouds

Dan Ruttle is my name, the name I will be called by all my life, even though it doesn't seem to belong to me. It's my father's name, and his father's name, my great grandfather Hector John Ruttle, the stone-mason. 'Mste 'Truttle's not in,' my mother says to casual visitors. My father hiding, sunbathing, keeping clear of visitors.

'Me Fawdur,' I manage to say, 'me Mudder,' 'and me Brudder.' Nothing can improve my accent. I am caught, trapped. My country accent depresses me. 'De Tams,' I say in school. The teacher looks out the window. It's a big river. Soho is under the ground, where gangsters from Glasgow fight with razors in the peaks of their caps.

I detest my accent, the slurred sound of it, nothing much would ever come of it. I hate my upbringing as I hate my match-stick arms and skeleton's legs, forever with sores or scabs, bleeding. I hate my rustic ignorance.

'Iffen,' I say.

'Fo mi fawdor,' I say to the cheeky girl in the shop. Her head ducks behind a biscuit tin. I see a ladle stuck in an open sack of meal. I hold the hot coin in my hand. The cheeky girl reaches over with her bare arm.

I think often of the Forbidden Place.

I go there, trespassing, walking amid broken branches, lost opportunities, the quick life that I can never grasp. Rotten branches break under my feet. I am hampered always by the dreadful timidity of adolescence. The cross-cut bites and the tree topples. A hand-axe is stuck into the chopping-block; the beheaded pullet attempts to run, it collapses, blood pours from its severed neck. On the block its eyes glaze. The rabbit chokes to death in the snare. Under the protective gauze I see the cold side of beef. I see a line of snares. It begins to snow. In

38

the night the rabbit chokes itself in my snare.

There is a rabbit in a snare in a circle of dirty earth. I kill it with a cricket stump. In the winter I collect dry kindling in Slish Wood. On the last Sunday of July I walk in procession to the shrine at Tobernalt. The nearness of tittering schoolgirls disturbs me. There have been no girls in the Ruttle line for over seventy years, my mother says.

'Daff'la wants a gude puck in the gob for himself!' the red-headed Carey boy says. Streams of snot pour from each of his nostrils, the gingery hair on his neck stands erect like the ruff of a dog, he throws off his jacket and shirt to expose a white chest and arms glistening with stringy labouring-man muscle. He squares up to me. How far will I go, the Garavogue dreamer? A ring forms. He comes at me like a mad dog. 'Take coward's blow!' I hear. A hard fist strikes at me as I strike back, feel something go in the freckled face, taste blood.

I who will always be a dreamy reserved unhappy sort of boy run with the rough lads out of the wood, pursued by grey-faced keepers. We hear them beating and halooing to each other in the depths of the wood. We are free by the river.

Carey cocks his leg and farts.

Fresh turds smoke on the moss under the trees. Carey can make curlicues and straight lines, even dots, with his steaming excrement, a rare gift. 'A fairies' football match,' he says, wiping himself with grass.

Wally and I attend garden parties given by the sons of the gentry. I sit tongue-tied, afraid to open my mouth. I am as much a failure with one party as with the other, accepted by neither the Careys nor the Wards. And, if reluctantly by the Orrs and Ruttles, never by the Gregories or the Gore-Booths. The things that make for life seem far away and quite beyond my reach, not in the country at all perhaps, not in Ireland.

'I don't play with girls,' Carey says, 'not with those soft little balls.' Looking down, I see wild drawings on the sand. The incoming tide fills the marks made by the sticks. 'P. Ray rode Kate Boyle' is wiped away. Carey's remark puzzles me. What do girls keep hidden under their skirts? The harbour turns cool as a cloud covers the sun.

I follow the footsteps of my maternal grandmother Nelly Orr who wears calfskin boots and an enveloping brown costume. We go into the living-room. She asks me what I would like to drink, knowing full well what I want. A maid brings in a siphon of lemonade and Gold Grain biscuits.

I follow my maternal grandfather along a narrow footbridge over the Shannon. Towards the mouth, its estuary, it must resemble Russia. Through paths in the high reeds men and women are walking, often alone. In the distance, smoke is ascending. All is hazy. My grandfather wears polished boots and a winged collar, a waistcoat under his buttoned tweed jacket, a watch and chain. The tributary hammers its waters through the sluices below me. I can see my grandmother waving from the bank. My grandfather offers me his hand.

Now we have a tutor. 'An animal that lives in a stable,' he says. 'It has four legs.' Wally and I look at each other. Our parents stand in the doorway. 'Don't be afraid to answer,' my father urges. 'It begins with a H,' the tutor says.

'A rat?' Wally whispers.

The tutor says that Wally will go far. Wally blushes. He blushes easily. Around his nose the skin turns white and around his eyes the skin goes red, when he strains, strains, with constipation. He is often constipated. 'Put vaseline on it,' he whines.

I lie down on the sofa. It's raining. I listen to it raining. I feel a great hole behind me and within me. I am on the Shores of Sleep. I hear a voice singing. It's John McCormack. I am caught in a slow troubled dream. When day ends my true life begins. I fall asleep as if I am being drawn slowly out of myself. Waking is hard. Grasp all, lose all. The days are slow to begin. I hear cocks crowing. My useless dreams *adhere to* me, fix me. I cannot escape. I watch Wally making progress, his notebooks filling up, he understands all that he is told. I understand nothing, or very little. I lag far behind. Will I ever catch up? I do not know myself.

My mother patiently explains to me that we two will be given opportunities to better ourselves and that we are privileged in that respect, compared to the local lads, and that we must put that advantage to use; she says we must not look down on them.

My mother is hidden in thick smoke, grey-white smoke that issues thickly from sodden burning leaves. I see the red-tail-light of a caravan in the smoke. It's Uncle Jack. The vagabond, voyager, egg-sucker has returned.

It's Sunday in Sligo. It's snowing on Ben Bulben. It's raining in Bundoran. I am in Drumcliff. It's Sunday in Sligo. I wander about in a controlled dream. No, in the dream that controls me. I see snow on Ben Bulben. Rooks circle. It's freezing. I throw skimmers on the ice.

'The Postman's Knock' is difficult to do on the long slide where buckets of water have been thrown on the road the night before.

I am running, I am on it, down on my hunkers and turning, keeling over. I come down on the slide, I am bleeding. Carey jumps on it with hobnailed boots and goes sailing down, turning slowly, with a look of fixed amazement. I am happy. Snow sparkles on the wall. But real life has not yet begun.

A long slobber hangs drooling from the mouth of a sick heifer. My father says that the animal will die. At once it recovers. 'Extraordinary,' my father says, washing his hands.

I take off my pyjamas and hide behind the bedroom door. I hear my father coming upstairs to say good-night to us. Bending down I open my behind, looking backwards through my legs. My father comes upside-down into the bedroom as Wally runs naked downstairs carrying a duster. 'That's not nice,' my father says. 'Put on your pyjamas.' I put on my pyjamas. We were playing at being Savages, pretending to be Fuzziwuzzis.

'He's just over-excited,' my mother says.

'We were only being Fuzziwuzzis,' I say lamely, knowing I had gone too far.

Wally, stark naked and with boot-blacked face, is beating a chamber-pot in the shrubbery.

'Get your brother in,' my father says in an exhausted voice.

'If they didn't know they were doing wrong, then they did no wrong,' my mother says. She tucks me into bed, kisses me on the cheek.

If there was one thing my mother abhorred it was 'showing off' or 'putting on airs'. Consequential little articles put on airs. Notice boxes showed off. She was very much down on all this. Or on devious carryings-on, particularly of a female nature. Miss Notice Box was a 'slithery article'. My mother disapproved of female cousins and nieces, and would not have them around the place. They were all Minxes, or 'underhand'.

'By all accounts,' my mother says. And: 'If all fruit fails.'

I hear girls cries in the shrubbery and the bamboos being shaken and a high excited female voice calls out 'He's over here!' Singing Polly Wolly Doodle-all-the-day (with her curly eyes and her laughing hair).

'No—over here!' another calls.

'Over *here*!'

'Over *where*?'

Bamboos are being buffeted. I am hidden in a place where no one will find me. I can move like a fox. No one can ever find me. I walk slowly back into the house. I hear the girls crying out in the plantation. Maeve Healy is now wearing trousers and a blouse you can almost see through. Parties with the sons and daughters of Landed Gentry are wilder

42

than parties with the rough boys, who do not know how to play. Derek Chapman, who wants to join the Royal Navy, arranges games of barricades, using cricket stumps, stones and air-guns. Rocks and air-gun slugs fly.

My father, tired of assisting me with arithmetic, draws a man's face in profile with streams of snot pouring from each nostril, on the back cover of my exercise-book. He draws always his own face, his long nose. He writes:

Miss Dolly Hart,
She let a fart,
Put it in a tin . . .

He puts his thumbs into his ears, rotating his hands so that his tongue comes and goes in and out, in and out. He crosses out the third line and writes instead:

She tied it to a string,

'Go on, Da,' I urge. 'Go on. What happened then?' My father chews the end of his pencil. I see that the profile he has drawn is his own face. He has an inspiration. He smiles as he writes:

She put in Miss C's house.
And let one out again!

Miss C. is Miss Coyle. She has a race-horse called 'One Down'. She lives in the back lodge. 'One Down' lives in our stables. My father and mother communicate in code during meals, referring to Miss C. and Mr H. and Mrs L. Most of these initials we can put names to.

'Are you any good in class?' my father asks me. 'Do the Sisters slap?'

'SumtimesdedoDa,' I say, feeling low as a worm. 'Sumtimes dedo.'

In church the Sister with the bad temper looks different, tranquil and holy under a black veil. The class of First Infants sing all together:

Deep in Thy wounds, Lord.
Hide and shelter me:

The tabernacle door is open. A breeze, from the habits of

the slowly passing nuns, touches me. My eyes are closed. It's Perpetual Adoration.

Closing my eyes again I feel the Eucharist dissolve in my mouth. Putting the tips of my fingers together I cross my thumbs and lower my head until my nose touches the index finger, I rise upwards slowly at the same time, and then backwards from a kneeling position, and move sideways away from the communion rail with closed eyes.

So shall I never,
Never part from Thee!

One of the big girls instructs us in Catechism, at the back of the class. I smell ink in the ink-well, the smell of the scored and stained wooden desk, the smell of the big girl. Lowering her head so that I smell her abundant auburn hair she whispers: 'Do you think you know it now?'

'Yes,' I whisper back; but I do not know it, and will never know it.

I mitch from school. I go with the rough lads to steal apples, show them the hole in the hedge that guards the orchard. I have made it myself from inside. It's our orchard at Nullamore.

'Wood'jer owlfellah mind? say ekum an'kotchus?'

'No,' I lie, 'no.' I am one of the lads.

Blazing red as beetroot, clasping a moth-eaten rug about him, his arms gleaming with linseed oil, and incoherent with rage at being disturbed while 'getting a colour up', my father stands up to his waist in the orchard grass and shakes a fist at Carey, caught red-handed up an apple tree. My father wears on his head an oil-stained handkerchief knotted at four corners. He comes leaping through the long grass, clasping the rug around his loins, waving his fist and crying out 'I'll . . . I'll . . .'

My father sits at table, crosses his legs. He wears tennis shoes and cut-down trousers, a sleeveless woollen jumper, his face red as rhubarb.

44

'Carey, a bloody little day-light robber, like his father before him.'

I pretend to be innocent.

My father is a Vet. His father was a farmer, and *his* father a stone-mason, dead before I was born. Daniel John Ruttle son of Daniel James Ruttle son of Hector John Ruttle stone-mason, of Sligo.

In the heavy family album my grandfather Hector appears as a big-boned humourless man with a long oxen jaw over a hard starched collar, bewhiskered as a Boer. My mother is the sweet-faced young woman in a wide-brim sunhat posing with her pretty sisters in the hay. The fiercely corseted hour-glass figure by the sundial at Jamestown is my grandmother Nelly Orr. 'Nothing,' my mother likes to repeat, 'ever got the better of your grandmother.' When almost ninety she still wrote a distinguished copperplate hand. Phlegmatic, like all the Orrs. 'My dear Dilly: I expect you know . . .'

The sun comes through the red blind in the study and dust motes rise. Our tutor writes on the blackboard in chalk:

Amo	amamus
amas	amatis
amat	amant

'Genutive singular,' the tutor says and points. Wally nods his head. His notebooks fill up. He is making progress. I am lagging. Wally sings 'I'm a rambler, I'm a gambler, I'm a long way from home, and if you don't like me just leave me alone.'

Stand in the garden at Wine Street, listen to the silence.

I collect cigarette cards, Wally collects stamps. I read Micky Mouse Annual. Wally reads Tom Webster's Annual and Pop. I read The Beano, The Dandy, Hotspur, Wally reads Lyn Doyle, Zane Gray.

An actor with a strange complexion and thigh boots, scarf knotted about his high-coloured neck, marches across the stage holding a double-barrel shot gun. With alarming noise

45

he discharges both barrels from the castle window. 'It's love,' Lizzy Bolger says, hot as a furnace sitting between us. 'That fella loved that wan.'

In the marquee at the matinee shadowy grey forms move on the screen. We watch Joe E. Brown in 'The Six Day Bicycle Race' and Charlie Chaplin in 'The Rink'.

My mother says that Chaplin is vulgar.

CHAPTER V

The Old Bishop, Crook'd Noonan

I turn twelve. I am said to be deceitful. Perhaps I am; I hardly know myself. I take Confirmation. Now I am supposed to be not only a 'strong' but also a 'perfect' Christian. I know otherwise. Perhaps I am a hypocrite. We were told to shout out the answers. The old Bishop is deaf. Colfer roars out the wrong answer at the top of his voice, as if the old Bishop was standing with his crozier and chrism on a hillside miles away. The old Bishop smiles and rests his anointed hand on Colfer's cropped head.

Sister Rumold says she is 'destroyed' by that fellow Ned Colfer.

The Tuppenny Catechism has a green cover and the questions are longer, the answers harder, more complicated. We move from the nuns over the river to the Christian Brothers, from the strap to the stick.

I stand on the south bank of the Garavogue. I smoke Wild Woodbines bought in open packets of five for tuppence. My father backs horses. I wait at the station for the arrival of the evening papers and cycle home with the *Herald* and the *Mail* rolled up together. *The Irish Times, Irish Press* and *Daily Mail* are delivered each morning, 37 papers in a week; my father takes 7 or more English Sunday newspapers. He plays golf at Strandhill off a handicap of 5.

I walk with Dicky Hart through the meadow near the quarry. We see Noonan running across a field, breaking through a wire fence. He runs, shaking his hook, which has replaced his right hand, shot off in the Boer War. He shouts: 'Off my land!' We run. I hear behind us the enraged shout, which comes to me as 'Off with my hand!' We run for our lives. I see him reflected in the depthless water of the quarry, running and waving his crook at us like Long John Silver.

Single-handed he built his own bungalow, sowed wheat. He will not tolerate anybody trespassing across his land, never. Then we are over the low wall and onto the road. We see him walking slowly back to his bungalow. From the chimney smoke is rising.

On St. Stephen's Day the Wren Boys come to the front door of Nullamore to sing:

The wran, the wran,
The king of all birds,
On St. Stephen's Day he was cotch in the furze;
So up with the kettle and down with the pan,
To hell with O'Duffy and Dev is your man!

My father gives them sixpence each.

'Are the Brothers hard? Do they use the stick?' my father asks me. As before he had said: 'There'll be bigger boys. Can you box your corner?'

'Can you box your corner?' Miss Hart asks. She cuts my hair and Wally's. I have a sheet around my neck. Sometimes my knees touch the thighs of the lady hairdresser. I smell her fingers. Short hairs go down my back. She holds out a hand-mirror. 'Would you fight your match?'

This is something I must understand and grasp. Not only the play with conkers, yos-yos, games in the wood, but this too. I go to early Mass. In winter it's dark, the road is a tunnel lit by the carbide light. The carbide fizzes. Hundreds of festive candles burn on the altar in the Cathedral.

'You must prepare yourself to receive our Lord,' the nun says. Sister Rumold is calm now. I move in a trance.

'Any excuse for swigging in bars,' my mother says. She refers to 'lounge-bar lizards', and I see my father drinking whiskey with a curious scaley creature who wears a midnight blue suit with razor-sharp creases, sipping some green concoction from a long-stemmed glass, sitting with legs crossed on a tall bar-stool, smoking a cigarette in a long holder while observing my father through the smoke with slit-eyes.

The eyes of Maria Montez flash dangerously, she wears a transparent dress. Sabu has curly lips and rides on an elephant. A trapdoor opens. Below, water, rats, sewers, nameless filth, a hideous fate. Streets are obscured in ground-fog, murderers are abroad. An old man—an Italian—plays a violin. 'Luigi has found it!' I try not to cry. I feel sick in my stomach. Melancholy overwhelms me.

Bunty Doyle shows home-movies. A rowing-boat approaches a wooden jetty by moonlight, in silence but for the whirr of the projector (I imagine I can hear the oars). A mysterious passenger shrouded in an overcoat, face shadowed under the brim of his hat, bends forward, his gaze fixed on the rower. The prow touches the jetty, the rower rises, begins to turn. Before I can see his face the film ends. It has no beginning and no end. Who are these men? Where do they come from? What are they doing?

Savages run through thick vegetation down a jungle path, a hunter drags a bear from a cave, Bunty Doyle lets off fireworks from the front railings, and coloured stars fall over Nullamore.

Wally and I leave the Capital, going down the marble steps past the cash-desk and the framed pictures of Robert Taylor and Madeleine Carroll, passing via the side-entrance into the Metropole next door where the commissionaire has tickets for us, and we go right into the middle of another film, the most secret and erotic dream come true, as Madeleine Carroll takes off her stockings behind a screen. A mouse runs up Wally's leg under his new 'longers'. Wally seizes it, pulls it out, drops it over the balcony rail, as with strained anxious faces Madeleine Carroll and Sterling Hayden meet in a cave under the sea, away from the sunlight with no disturbance or interruption possible. The Cave Under the Sea! I want to see it all again. The curtains part once more like an aurora borealis.

'The roars and the bawls of them,' old Jem Brady says, 'you'd think they were men,' referring to the Charter School girls running on the hockey field.

'Above all the birds in the air,' old Jem Brady says, 'I do hate a rat.'

One day he is taken stiff out of the depthless waters of the quarry. Dressed in a monk's habit he lies in a trestled coffin at the back of the Cathedral. Essy Brady goes weeping over the bridge. I cycle into the village for the evening papers, and the tyres whisper that old Jem Brady is dead. A blue light hovers over the quarry.

CHAPTER VI

The Gulf of Dreams

Wally stands before me, abject. Abject his manner, abject his mien.

'Quite honestly Sir,' he says in an affected high fluting English accent, 'I'd feel much better after a jolly good hiding.'

'Right, my boy,' I say heavily. 'Right, Walter.'

Wally raises his eyes to me as if beseeching. He is the errant son. I am the heavy inflexible father, about to administer the father and mother of a thrashing. 'A good licking,' Wally whispers.

'Bend down, boy.'

Wally holds his knees. The cane is raised high.

'Now, Sir.'

The cane smashes down on the desk. Again, again.

'Yarooh!'

'You're looking pasty,' my mother says.

I am dosed with cascara. I eat tapioca and sago which is like irogspawn. Now it's Wally's turn to look pasty. He is Malcolm Cambell, then Napoleon. In the ritual flogging the cane is broken. I cut another from the bamboos, whistling 'Two Lovely Black Eyes'. Wally rolls on the tennis court, marking his trousers, kicking fat legs in the air.

'Whelps,' my father says, smiling.

My father's heroes are Jammy Clinch, Tommy Conniff, Stanley Woods, Napper Tandy.

My mother's idols are Anthony Eden, Noël Coward and Beverley Nichols.

Wally's heroes are Tilden, Vines, Budge, Bobby Riggs.

My heroes are: Teddy Lester, Ito Nagao, Arthur Digby.

'Ah, feck,' I say; it dribbles out of my mouth against my wish. 'Fecking,' I say, hating the word and myself. Fecking-this, fecking-that.

'Poo,' I say. 'Smelly poo.'

Wally is obstinate, set in his ways ('thick,' my mother says). His ambition: to be a bird. A crow, for instance.

Malcolm Cambell is breaking the world record in his Blue Bird. Wally takes his model of the Blue Bird to bed with him, races it on the covers.

'Garters,' Wally says. 'Golly!'

I think of Gina's garters and blush.

Garters!

'The dibs,' my father says. 'The dough . . .' ('When the dough runs out'). When it arrives we'll be rolling in money.

Josey Darlington vamps on his Hohner harmonica. He is short of breath, he wheezes, he has asthma. He plays 'Finiculi Finicula' and then 'The Isle of Capri'.

A deceptive delivery swings to the left of me and Wally holds up his arms to high Heaven. He is Headley Verity, his attack is unplayable.

'Hard cheese.'

Virol, Oxo cubes, eggflips, Bisto.

'The yellow bittern!' Wally says giving a highpitched laugh.

The shores of sleep. The gulf of dreams.

CHAPTER VII

The Old Man on the Mall, Ned Colfer, the Tunny Shoals

I do not hate my body. I touch it. I like to touch it. But the priest says: 'Do not touch yourself. Do not play with yourself.'

'Listen to what the priest says,' the old nuns say.

'What is "adultery"?' I ask in all innocence.

The old nun looks at me with red-rimmed eyes.

'What does it mean, Sister?'

'Don't ask that question! Don't you dare ask that!' She gives the desk a knock with her knuckles. 'Adultery's a crime!' she cries, pushing me in the back.

Molly Cushen, in a gym-slip too small for her, is forbidden to play with her skipping-rope. 'Molly can give it a few twirls,' the old nun says. 'But no skipping or jumping.'

The big girls are taught in a classroom at the bottom of the school yard. I walk in procession behind the big girls. In a clearing in the wood before an open-air altar the priest raises the heavy gold monstrance. The rose chasuble glows like fire, incense rises from the thurible, the gravel bites into my knees. Benediction is endless. I smell incense, powder, cosmetics, the wood. The wind sighs in the trees. Evening draws on. It turns cool. I think of cold roast well salted, dry bread.

Behind the golf pro's hut the wild young caddies remove Mary Moore's drawers. She has a brown mole on her thigh. She is ten. Mattie Green holds her down. She struggles like a fish. 'For two pins I'da gev her a few squirts,' Mattie says.

'A rub'ada relic!' the wild boys shout, all together. 'Over the bar with Lowry Maher! . . . Areesh!' They begin to wrestle on the ground. Then the maroon drawers sail over the hut.

I cycle to school. One Irish mile. I see plover in the cold drills. Wally and I leave our bikes behind the spare counter in Mrs King's shop. We buy three-tier cakes. The shop has a nice smell.

Sister is calm now. I move in a trance. We pass through the open iron side-gate into the Cathedral where all the statues are shrouded in purple.

Sister Rumold the little crabby old nun offers my mother a Zube to suck in the parlour of the convent. The Zubes are in a tin box shaped like a bar of soap.

'My sons are different,' my mother says, both timid and proud. The old nun looks at Wally and I, slowly nodding her head, her lips pressed together on a Zube. They discuss our education. 'Education is so important, these days,' my mother says. She is dressed like a grand lady. She smokes. Wally and I are to go to Killashee prep school, run by a French order of nuns, if the National School does not 'work out'. All are terrified of Brother O'Mahon, who uses the stick. The Brothers believe in beating.

I cycle home from Mass with frozen fingers. Old Mrs Henry puts my hands into steaming water, I cry. I eat gruel. The days are short now. The evening light shines over old Ben Bulben. I see crows tossed about in the wind. Days are cold. We are to move to the National School. Our fate has been decided.

'Your pal,' my mother says, smiling. 'What does your pal say?' meaning the old man who sits on a bollard on the Mall all day long. I am often with him. I smoke a clay pipe. He gives me fills of shag tobacco, paring it slowly towards his thumb.

'The munts,' he says, 'the yeers,' 'the lurry,' 'the wurrdild.' Smelling of tobacco, old clothes, he makes all seem both far away and near, both perfectly formed and twisted, both exact and forlorn. With him I feel at peace.

'Stand up now, Ned Colfer,' Brother O'Mahon orders.

'Spell "patriotism" for us.'

Pulling a woeful face and with head down and eyes closed Colfer begins stuttering.

'Now Ned, take your time.'

'Pat-pat-pat . . .' Colfer stutters, gulping, choking, drowning.

'Take your time,' Brother O'Mahon says, smooth as silk, taking hold of the cane. Colfer looses his head, begins again.

'Pee- pee- pee . . .'

Brother O'Mahon looks out of the window with a long-suffering face. Crows are flying by, free as air, bound for the stubble-fields, their liberty. The classroom smells of damp clothes. The lessons are hard. First Infants seem far away, the convent playground, Sister Rumold.

'Po- po- po . . . ppppp,' Ned Colfer says, with eyes closed tight, gobbling like a turkey.

'Very well,' Brother O'Mahon says, moving towards Colfer. 'Spell "stupidity" for me.'

'Stew- stew- stew . . . Sssppp—'

The cane crashes down on the desk.

'I'll stew-stew you!' Brother O'Mahon cries in a high voice. '*I'll* stew-stew you, you dolt. Stand out here!'

Ned Colfer holds out a trembling hand at an awkward angle. Brother O'Mahon touches it, steadies it, raises the cane high. Colfer averts his face.

I long for the open, the fields. Class is endless. The Maynooth Catechism is hard, Irish is hard, the days are long. I hear the river running out under the broken floorboards. Brother O'Mahon unrolls a worn-looking map of Ireland.

The old man on the Mall likes to puzzle me. He tells of the tunny shoals migrating off the Azores and Dogger Bank, passing north of Scotland, making their way into Irish estuaries and rivers to their old spawning grounds, a journey that could be shortened by a third if they had the sense to use the English Channel. But, coming this way since before the waters broke through, when Great Britain and Ireland were one with Europe in one great land-mass, they knew no better, still using the old sea-route. Did I not know? What did I make of that?

Then you could walk from Sligo over to Paris, down to Vienna?

'Storm-water,' the old man says, pointing out to sea where seagulls were wheeling over sewage. Vapoury blue eyes look askance at me from under tufted eyebrows. I'd never *heerd*, never know, I smell tobacco, an old man's clothes that he never changes. He reaches out to hold me.

'No.'

'What do-dey taych ye in skule—innything useful?' I smell an old man who lives alone. He holds me between his knees. I feel his bones.

'No.'

I stand away. The old man spits shag mixed with spit between his legs.

The lame pumping stroke sounds in the front yard. Father is filling the tank. The wheel is loose, the platform unsteady, it takes an hour's labour to fill the water tank on the roof. My father pumps resentfully, conserving himself, often stopping. The land steward Tommy Flynn generally does the pumping. Sometimes the dairyman. Sometimes the Bowsy Murray in his waistcoat. My father complains of persistent aches and pains, darts of sciatica, twinges of lumbago, shoots of arthritis, or *desperate* darts of this and that ailment, striking when (and where) least expected, but generally attacking at pumping-time, when I cycle to the village for the evening papers, Mutt and Jeff. The old appendix is at him again, it is killing him, pumping was absolutely out of the question.

He had a growth under one ear, a kind of goitre. He had been persuaded, after years, to go into hospital and have it removed. But there his nerve had failed him. Knotting bed-sheets together he made his escape by night, walking home in dressing-gown and slippers. Wild horses would not drag him back there. The surgeon was a bloody butcher. He was lucky to escape alive.

'The Ruttles were all like that,' Nelly Orr says. 'Afraid of the knife.'

CHAPTER VIII

The Ring-Pump, Dublin Zoo, Oscar

'Dying gad,' my mother says. 'When all fruit fails.' 'A lug.' 'A wreck.' 'Consequential.' 'Giddy, brainy, hefty. A Yahoo.'

'Nancy-boys,' my father says, pursing up his lips. 'Nancy sopranos.'

What do these words mean?

I comb my mother's long hair, tell her of Charlie Chaplin in 'The Rink', Joe E. Brown in 'The Six Day Bicycle Race', both of which I have seen at a matinee in the marquee on a pale screen. I suck boiled sweets. My mother's long brown hair smells nice. The paraffin lamp gives out a white glow, my father reads Mutt and Jeff, both feet up against the mantelpiece. He cuts the backs out of shoes, cuts trousers short below the knees, around his neck he wears knotted handkerchiefs. We take candles into the dark bedroom where the wind booms, blows the candle out. I crawl into bed, between chilly sheets, struggle towards sleep, hear Wally already snoring.

A sheep runs in my dreams with its head half-eaten off. It runs bleeding and baa-ing, pursued by an Alsatian hound turned wolf. A sleigh piled up with furs is pulled at breakneck speed through a pine forest by terrified horses, pursued by a pack of wolves. Bearded men gesticulate and flog the horses onward. It's Russia.

On the borders of my father's seventy-two acre estate the ring-pump is out of order, has long been so, and the boards that cover it are rotten. Dangerous to walk over rotten boards. Grass grows on the stone trough and in the channels of the overflow: the pump itself has rusted stiff.

I look down into the well. Twenty feet below, and inverted, I see upside-down clouds and in them my face.

58

Both are reflected in trembling water. I spit into the well. My face breaks up when the spit hits the water, the clouds disappear. Then face and sailing clouds are back. Some animal has drowned there, hare or cat. It lies face down and bloated, its backbone breaking through the split skin as the carcass continues to fall apart. In the shallow well-water I see an intently observing face above a tyreless bicycle and a zinc chamber pot with the bottom perished. The bones of the animal will in time sink, survive longer. I move away.

'Hey!' Wally says. 'What's the big idea?' I stand below him in a ditch. He points at the mark where the snowball struck his leg, his turn-ups are filled with snow. 'Take that out,' he orders. I do as I am bid.

Little by little, day by day, the years go by.

This little piggy went to market,
This little piggy stayed at home . . .

becomes

Goosey, Goosey Gander, where do you wander?
Upstairs and downstairs and in my lady's chamber .

Which in time becomes

Georgie-Porgie, pudding and pie,
Kissed the girls and made them cry.

In the old times a chamber was a bedroom. A chamber is also a po-pot. In the maid's uncarpeted room, smelling its smells of poverty and dust, old Mrs Henry's po is filled to overflowing with orange-coloured pee.

George Henry, our cook's big son, cuts his hand, a deep cut. He runs cold water on it from the tap, puts salt in it. Cowboys put moss in their wounds.

Helen O'Connor takes Wally and I to the Dublin Zoo in her Baby Austin. All day I feel uncomfortable, sick with excitement. The monkeys pull faces, jump on their swings, a long snake lies in a tree, the lions sleep. The journey home is endless. At last the car door is open and an excited pekinese jumps onto the back seat, I vomit in the hall.

Dr O'Connor wears a cravat below a goatee beard, parts

59

his hair in the middle, wears spats. Muffled up in a long fur coat he drives about the countryside at ten miles an hour in an old Rolls Royce. He keeps human skulls in his cellar. Helen O'Connor wears glasses. She reads banned books, lends them to my mother. I read Philip Gibbs.

Opposite the underground toilets in the Grafton Cinema, the homesteaders of the midwestern plains regard me. They have gnarled hands, their faces much creased, wind-blown, all blue-grey. Pedestrians walk on the stippled glass over my head. I look at the grey-blue company. They cluster together, stare back at me. *'Soon it will be their turn.'* What does that mean? Theirs a hard life, they are coming to the end of it. Helen O'Connor smokes while she drives. I feel ill. Home at last. Lizzy Bolger comes across the hall. 'You're wanting,' she tells me. I try to think of a phrase that will include all my misery, my life.

Logan-berries and rasberries grow against the garden wall, near the pear trees, heavy clods of earth are turned, cabbage planted, peas cultivated, hens stray in from the back yard, Wally keeps records, eggs collected, hens brooding. In the open cess-pit thick white maggots and worms squirm in an unspeakable stench. Near the wood a dead sheep lies. The air around is black with blue-bottles, seen in the dead skull as gleams of phosphorescent viridian. Corruption is like tar or treacle. The ants are in the currants, the wasps in the apples, fruit-flies in the plums. Oscar the Alsatian escapes from his cage, eats half the head off a sheep; it lies near the hedge, still alive, with a crown of flies. My father beats Oscar with golf-sticks, not using the handles. Oscar howls like a wolf. The air hums.

CHAPTER IX

Country Circus

The stained canvas of the marquee slaps against its braced supports, sinking and rising as if taking great deep breaths, as the winds drag at it. Inside, a band plays. Fossett's Circus has come again to Sligo. It's in a field near the sea.

The band, huddled on a makeshift rostrum, plays old airs, circus tunes. The trampled grass smells of damp earth. A white-faced clown with a bulbous red nose and orange hair stumbles in big boots and baggy pants across the ring to fall into the lap of an embarrassed countrywoman sitting in the first tier of wooden seats. He begins to bawl, calling her Ma. The audience roars, laughing and jeering.

Obscene is the stare of the clown, joking with the audience, raising his eyebrows, cocking one leg. Obscene the angle and position of the flower he carries. He walks with a slowness amounting to criminal intent, his gestures licentious in the extreme. He seems to have wet himself or done it into his pants, he lifts both feet, examines the soles of his boots, looks into his trousers. Opening his mouth wide he sticks out an astonishing tongue. He shouts at the tired band. The crowd love him. He is everywhere, holding it all together with coarse innuendos.

Wally and I sit with our Da in the best seats.

A yokel with bad teeth holds onto a bucket near the point where the animals make their entrances and exits. A Lion Tamer doubles as Strong Man. Bare to the waist he cracks his whip to make the jungle killers lay back their ears. The lioness emits a blood-curdling growl and slinks along the bars. The lions sit on tall tubs and yawn at the audience. The Lion Tamer lies on the fierce lioness and feigns sleep. Then he kisses the lioness. Fellows in boiler suits drag the cage out and in come the performing dogs, followed by a female dog-trainer in riding costume bursting at the hips. She moves with a bouncy walk. The dogs are all over the place. I watched the jauntily swaggering hips of the trainer.

But the bare-back rider who comes next sweeps all before her. The band, brightening up, plays her signature tune, and in she comes.

First she circles the ring astraddle two trotting ponies. Her actressy eyes catch the light. She holds her bare arms out. I see her spine and rounded knees as she goes through a blazing hoop. She is all movement, all mystery, strikes no poses, demands no applause, and is beautiful beyond words.

Two dusty white ponies with red plumes circle the ring. Her strong thighs, her calmness, agility, as she leaves one broad back for the encircling barrier, leaves it for the other broad back, facing forward, then backward, is something to see. The Ringmaster points his long whip at her, following her progress in a smaller circle, he is speechless. At the finale she joins him, he has his arm about her, his top hat off, demanding applause. He even helps to chase the ponies out of the ring. From their short trotting legs to their nodding plumes they are all jogging movement, advancing in time to the music, out of Time. The young rider seems to drift. She walks over them, through them, flows onto the barrier, the music ends in a flourish. She runs off.

Wild horses come in at full gallop with a handler being dragged off his feet by their maddened progress, pulling at the traces for dear life. The handler shouts 'Hup-hup, hup-hip!' The big horses tear around. 'Hubblebay!' The band cannot keep up with them. The lions, pulled in again, are dragging their fur against the bars and pissing violently. Wally hisses between his teeth. All pass, the animals too. 'Alleyoop!'

Now, disguised as a Strong Man in a leopard skin which leaves half his chest bare, the Lion Tamer is back, on his feet Roman sandals, on his wrists leather straps with buckles.

Arching his back and puffing out his cheeks he lifts an impossible weight previously carried in by four men, two of them staggering.

The bare-back rider, now dressed, all demure in a raincoat, is selling raffle tickets between the rows of seats. Da buys raffle tickets from her. 'You never know, we may just be lucky,' he says, pocketing his change. I try not to look at her.

During the intermission, the Strong Man, changed into a dark blue suit with ox-blood shoes and an open-neck white shirt, talks to her by the entrance, flashing his white teeth. Under her raincoat she wears a short tulle skirt and Wellington boots. I see again her pleated underskirt and strong white thighs as she stands facing the wrong way on the pony's back, turning up her wrists, looking about her with bright actressy eyes, deep into her act, pulled hither and thither by the music, by the ponies, by the bay, by the turning earth itself. Nothing can sully her, not even the sallies of the red-nosed clown, who hates her. The Ringmaster walks in a tight circle with his long whip folded, as if witnessing perfection itself, never taking his eyes off her as she leaps through a whole series of hoops, and under electric light the marquee looks less shabby, the ponies whiter, brisker in their trotting, as a heavy shower of rain hits the side of the marquee, where an ostler stands with his mouth open, holding under one arm a bucket of sawdust and lion dung.

And now she has jumped from the back of the last pony for the last time and the Ringmaster had his arm about her waist again for the last time, and the ponies are running out by themselves, and the trumpeter is holding what appears to be a red chamber-pot before the mouth of his instrument, and the top of the marquee is slapping against the high poles, and the lights fixed around the ring are shining on the top hat of the Ringmaster and the eyes and teeth of the bareback rider, and then the last turn is over at last and the lights are being taken down and Lizzy and I are leaving among the last. I hear the tractor belt humming and there is the Strong Man on the steps of a caravan, talking to the bareback rider, now in a raincoat with a headscarf and fur boots. He talks to you. You bend your head and listen. They will travel all over Ireland together. Lizzy and I pass through the gate out of the circus field into pelting rain, and Lizzy asks me did I like it? Did I *like* it!

'Tha' fella does have me heart-scalded,' Lizzy tells her best friend Rita Phelan.

'Oh, let him go again, if it means so much to him,' my mother said to my father.

'Extraordinary,' Da said.

'I'm going to tell on you,' Rita Phelan says, spiteful.

'Me ould segochia!' Grogan says to me in the yard. His cruel cat-stretching hands seize me.

'Don't be at him, Grogan. You're always at him,' Lizzy says. But the cat-torturer's hands hold me in a vice.

The bare-back rider! the bare-back rider! Where would you find her equal in tights today?

CHAPTER X

The Bowsy Murray, Vimy Ridge and the King of England

The Bowsy Murray pushes his delivery bike up the front avenue of Nullamore. The gradient is too much for him. Every Saturday he brings a sirloin of beef wrapped in bloody paper in his butcher's basket. Old Mrs Henry offers him a bottle of Guinness when she has asked him to sit down and take the weight off his feet. The Bowsy Murray stinks up the kitchen.

'A nice piece of meat,' old Mrs Henry says with approval before carrying it off to the larder. The Bowsy Murray looks down complacently at his gaitered legs while Lizzy Bolger draws the cork for him. The Bowsy keeps his little finger out as he pours. He draws his fingers through his walrus moustache and brings up a low rumbling belch. 'Rift,' my mother calls it. The Bowsy first washes his hands with coarse soap at the tap. Old Mrs Henry hangs the big sooty kettle over the range. I hear the fire in the chimney. I put the poker through the bars and when it is red-hot I lay it across a slice of bread spread with brown sugar. I make a game of noughts and crosses. It tastes of treacle. Lizzy Bolger sings at the wash-tub:

> A-roamin' in the gloamin'
> By the bonny banks of Clyde . . .

'That stomach of yours must be wan mass of worms,' she says. I do not eat butter, put sugar on all my food, my stomach one mass of worms.

'No.'

Screwing up her eyes and tilting the empty teacup this way and that, old Mrs Henry begins to foretell the future in tea-leaves. The backs of her hands are freckled. Flecks of amber in pale blue eyes, strands of white in her grey hair she wears brown worsted stockings, has a funny smell. A nice smell. She sees dark strangers, journeys across water, good and bad fortune on the way. Her finger moves below lines of print, her lips move, she uses a hairpin to underline difficult words. The Italians are fighting the Abyssinians.

'Poor bloody savages,' the Bowsy says, putting down his Guinness.

Lizzy Bolger lowers the clothes-line. It's a long bar held in place against the ceiling by a rope looped about a stanchion by the mangle. Above it in bed at night I hear it come squeaking and gibbering down like the damned in distant Hell.

I walk on large paving-stones down a whitewashed corridor below the line of dusty bells. The walls are covered in drawings. In the kitchen, old Mrs Henry and Lizzy are cleaning and plucking beheaded pullets. Feet in feathers, hands bloodied, they pull out entrails, winking and sniggering like a couple of witches, their reddened hands methodically plucking feathers. I smell cold guts.

'Where's Ma?'

Silence. I stand at the door, watch them.

'Yewer Mammy's run off with a soldier,' Lizzy says at last. With the back of her hand she moves hair from her eyes, leaving a smear of blood on her forehead.

'No.'

'Yewe'll see, Mister Smarty.'

I run from the witches.

I am with the footballers in a clearing. The ball is sodden and heavy. The wet grass sparkles. Evening. The sun is sinking behind the trees. Rabbits come out along the ditch. We march through the wood singing,

> I stuck my nose up a nanny-goat's hole,
> The smell it nearly blinded me.

The little grey and white mother hen runs about, clucking at her brood, rooting backwards with her spurs. Subsiding on her under-feathers, the chickens burrow in, their small heads look out here and there, one on her back. Eyes glazing over, she settles herself in the dust for sleep.

Wally collects eggs, keeping meticulous records: hens who lay where they should lay, others who prefer to lay in ditches. Rats eat the eggs, or the chickens. Oscar, long unfed, grown thin and rapacious as a wolf, breaks out of his cage, eats chicks, eggs, hens, the rats.

Wally cuts out Irish XVs and XIs from *The Irish Times* and *Tatler & Sketch* and colours them, each player with the correct blazer or stockings, the giants with folded arms. Beamish and Crawford, Jammy Clinch who in India killed a man with his bare hands. Because he had crossed his path, my father said. Clinch certainly looked capable of anything. Once he had set fire to a train.

'Yewer Mammy's run off with a sailor!'
'Sick and tired of the pair of ye!'
'Too finickety!'
I escape from the kitchen.

A barrel-chested sailorman pulls steadily at the oars, smiling at my mother who sits facing him. She is dressed for a long journey. The sailor has red hair and green eyes; behind him a ship rides at anchor. My mother is leaving without a by-your-leave, without a backward glance. Up anchor at full tide! Choking with unhappiness I lie in the long smothering grass.

The Bowsy Murray tells me again of his time at war. One Sunday, following a week-long bombardment, he advanced with his company across a hill of blackened corpses into Vimy Ridge. The corpses had lain a week in the sun, killed in the shelling. I sit on the table.

'Lost in action,' the Bowsy says, pouring hot tea into the saucer and looking at me with a troubled eye. 'Glory be to God, some of them went out over the field in bits and pieces.

He tells me it all again. The explosion to the right or to

the left, the scream of pain (someone had bought it), the blow on the chest over the heart, the air over Vimy Ridge turning grey. 'Anything wrong, Gunner Murray? Are you hit?' his officer asked. No, nothing wrong exactly, except the air was purple and blood already had begun to fill his boots.

He lies among the corpses, looking up at his officer. He is carried behind the lines on a stretcher. From field hospital to ship by troop-train across Belgium; the Irish wounded are returning home. Following a slow sea-voyage an unknown port is reached. From hold to a closed ambulance he is shifted. An orderly sits with the wounded, asks them: 'Any of you blighting Paddies got relatives 'ere?'

'Where are we?'

'Dublin.'

Dublin! Glory be to God, hadn't he a sweetheart in Ranelagh! Sitting up in a hospital bed, writing to her, a pair of hands reach over his shoulders and cover his eyes. Herself!

There is a hole in his chest, a sort of web covers it; dark blood from near the heart pumped out of it, but no doctor can find the shrapnel until Sir James Ware walks through the wards. Sir James makes a mark with an indelible pencil on his chest and tells him not to rub it out. The X-Ray shows the piece of shrapnel near the heart.

After the operation he marries, becomes a gamekeeper on Lord Portarlington's estate at Omu Park. He has two sons, a fine big house, sixty acres of land. He acts as gun-bearer for King George VI ('I knew him as well as I know your own Daddy').

I look down on the matted hair, the hands of the soldier who had been on Vimy Ridge, had walked with Lord Portarlington at Omu Park, handed a gun to the King of England. I try to imagine the Bowsy in puttees and uniform, a tin hat, carrying rifle and pack, going to fight for King and country, beating hares and pheasants towards the King whom he knows as well as he knows my own father. No doubt he tells the King, as he has told Wally and me, that the dead on that fateful Sunday were strewn about, Irish and English mixed, as 'numerous as the leaves' on the hedge behind him.

A few years pass. His sons grow up. One day, walking alongside a hay-bogey, the load shifts, and a pitch-fork goes through his knee. Nothing will persuade him to go to hospital; he has had enough of hospitals. (He and my father talk endlessly of this, or rather my father does, the Bowsy listens, nods his head, agrees with every word.) He suffers on and off for nine years. At the end of that time a Dublin surgeon cripples him for life.

The pain has come back too often, he cannot sleep, he decides to have it seen to. Given a choice between Dr Chance and Dr Cherry he makes the wrong choice. 'How long have you had these?' the surgeon asks, touching his varicose veins. 'We'll whip those lads out too.'

He is given sedatives and a 'hundred' injections, put to sleep and operated on. Convalescence is long. After five weeks he demands his clothes, but is told 'You go out of that door at your own peril, Murray.' He takes a train, walks three miles, reaches home. All is in disorder. A country buck is looking after the farm with one of his sons. They breed pigs; the country buck tends them, does the rough work. The Bowsy's temper has become erratic, putting his foot on the ground is 'like putting it into a furze bush'. One evening, while sitting down at supper, the sucks began screeching in the stye.

'What's the matter with the sucks?' he questions the country buck. The country buck looks at him around his shoulder. The sucks are hungry, fed only twice a week. 'Arrah why should I fade dim,' the country buck says. 'Isn't wance or twice a wake enough?'

The Bowsy rises straight up. His son blocks the doorway. 'Me son is as strong as a gate.' The Bowsy breaks past, has his knife out, goes for the sucks, intending to slit every throat

69

in the stye. The knife enters the side of the suck's neck as the Bowsy falls, tackled by his son; he comes to his senses. The suck is bleeding and screeching, the pig-stye in an uproar.

Lizzy sings in a phenomenally high voice, scrubbing the wash:

> When the sun sinks in the west
> That's the time that I love best . . .

I study the Bowsy; from him so generally reserved, who speaks most grudgingly, every so often comes this long yarn, the story of his escape on Vimy Ridge, his times with Lord Portarlington and the King of England.

He drinks Guinness in a circumspect way, his little finger crooked. He pours scalding tea into his saucer, slurps it up. I see tattoo marks on his arm, the same that took the injections before the unsuccessful operation. His sons have grown up.

He sells the house and lands at a loss, going next day to the auctioneers, after sacking the country buck, moves with his wife to Sligo and there begins a new life as a butcher's delivery-man and slaughterer.

He spreads sawdust on the shop floor, scrubs the chopping block, hoses down the yard—a close-mouthed man.

Now hoisting the empty basket onto the crook of his arm, he puts on his sweaty cap, bids old Mrs Henry and Lizzy the time of day and limps from the kitchen.

I watch him retreating down the front avenue, cranking down on the pedals, his shoulders crooked. He wears a blue-and-white apron. The butcher's shop is a mile away in the village. Cattle and pigs are driven towards it, sheep and lambs; wearing a sack about his waist the Bowsy herds them into the yard. Their blood runs down the drains. Does he whistle through his teeth as he sharpens the knife before doing in the poor creatures, as he does when waiting for his tea to cool? Sometimes on the wind I hear the irate highpitched screeching of stuck pigs.

'The Bowsy is reliable,' my mother says.
'I think the world of the Bowsy,' my father says.
What they mean is: Bowsy Murray knows his place.

Sunday bells chime from the Cathedral. I go into the
rockery for a blue flower for my button-hole. I wear my
Sunday suit of light blue tweed. I look at the foreign Mass
Card in my prayer book: a monochrome oval with Jesus
wearing a crown of thorns.

Ecce Homo
Ter mille van Une H. Wonden, a Jezus,
ontferm Uoner de arme zielen.

And on the obverse.

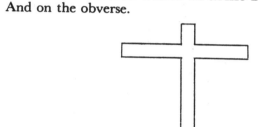

J.M.J.
Niet mijn wil, O Heer, maar de
uwe geschiede. (Luc. XXII, 42)
Bid voor de zial zaliger

Mijnheer
Gustaaf Juliann Ernst Moorkens
echtgenoot van Mevrouw
Florentina Carolina Pelgrims

geboren de Herenthals den 5 mei 1861 en aldaar zeer
godvruchtig overleden den 11 juni 1926, voozien de
H. H. Sacramenten der stervenden. Genadige Jesus, geef
zijne ziel de eeuwige rust.

71

I replace it in my white prayer-book, return to the house. Wally is waiting in the hall, adjusting each finger into brown leather gloves (in May!) with a judicious expression on his face. Old Mrs Henry and Lizzy Bolger go to early Mass. The Ruttles go to the latest Mass. Father prefers to arrive as late as possible, remain in the porch throughout, leave before the Last Gospel. My mother stays at home. Crowded places do not suit her; her nerves are bad—they frequently go 'against' her. A priest comes to hear her private Confession once a year and she receives Holy Communion next morning in bed, in a bedroom full of flowers.

From the Romanesque depths of the Cathedral, beyond the rising incense, the confusion as the congregation kneels, we hear the tintinnabulation of the little joined bells—the signal for my father to heave a reluctant sigh, spread a clean linen handkerchief, thrice folded, on the floor of the porch and get down on one knee, sinking his head into his spread fingers.

When the joined handbells have announced that the Consecration is over, my father sighs again, uncovers his eyes, stands, replaces his handkerchief in his breast pocket. I hear an outbreak of coughing and clearing of throats. The men in the porch tell their beads (action of shelling peas). As we leave I hear the priest's voice raised, warning of the wicked spirits who wander through the world for the ruin of souls. I know the Mass is ending. We do not wait for Benediction. The men in the porch, with a quick sideways dip of the knee, depart.

At times I enter the Cathedral, find a place, kneel. A Bishop with little or no hair on his head intones rapid Latin ('*Beebalongholiday*' it sounds like), bending forward and striking the stiff vestments over his breast while incense pours from the thurible. A man with false hair kneels before me. The flowers on the High Altar come from Nullamore. My mother is driven over each Saturday with the car full of flowers. Now it is pale purple lupins from the rockery, these are her prayers in absentia. Mrs Walshe helps her to arrange the flowers. Mrs Walshe takes tea and cakes at Nullamore. ('I'm full to the muzzle.')

My father donates generously at the collection. He makes a General Confession once a year at the Discalced Carmelite Church of St. Teresa in Dublin, flatly refusing to confess his sins to local priests who know 'too damned much already,' being for the most part narrow and bigoted men.

Instead he confesses behind a brown drape into the discreet ear of a Carmelite monk dressed in a brown habit. My father's confessions tended to be long affairs. Wally and I sit in the hushed church, hearing a harp play outside in Johnston's Court. I fall to wondering what adults might confess to, serious sins, hearing the wind humming in the organ loft, the sound of harp strings being plucked. Then we must wait for hours in the foyer of the Grafton Cinema.

Mr Shakespear the uniformed commissionaire keeps an eye on us. We sit in a seat near the cash-desk and speak in whispers. My father drinks in the Sign of the Zodiac or in the Shelbourne Hotel. An unfrocked clergyman with rotten teeth sits between us and says atrocious things in a low voice. We stand on the steps, feeling uncomfortable. Outside it is raining. 'A Hundred Men and a Girl' is still running. We look at the stills. The Grafton is patronised by protestant clergymen up from the country with their plain wives. Facing the underground toilets hangs a poster that troubles and fascinates me. A group of men and women with gnarled veined hands and cropped hair huddle together and stare out at me. They are blue-grey on a similar ground, people of the American Plains. The caption below says: '*Soon it will be their turn.*' I stand at the urinal, see feet passing above me, and wonder what this means, sick from fudge and ice-cream, my hair clipped short at Maison Prost and stuck to my scalp with stiffener. Their eyes follow me, bore into me. What are they thinking? Why do they stare at me?

We stand in a blue grotto lit by neon and a darkly visaged hawk-nosed Jewish assistant shows me a selection of Hohner mouth-organs in a glass case. My father pays, remarking on the weather, bad for the crops, untimely at this time of year. The Jewish salesman, who smells of scent and expensive cigarettes, agrees in a bored way. We leave Harris's Music Shop, my father talking all the way to the door. It's still raining outside, Mr Shakespear is holding up a coloured golf umbrella over the head of a small lady who cannot stop talking, and a line of ten or twelve wait in the downpour to see Deanna Durbin. Wally is buying stamps for his collection. My father appears, bringing us sketch pads from Woolworth's. In the Grafton Cafeteria we are served buttered bread, ham and tea. My father asks for dry bread and jam for me. Miss Nairn serves us. My father speaks of the weather, the crops. During the Emergency, when cigarettes will be scarce and rationed, she will put aside packets for my father, curious brands never seen before, Kerry Blue, Passing Clouds, black Turkish brands that suggest to me wantonness and lust. We hear city people passing below in the rain, talking and laughing. The city smells strange.

The Manager of the Grafton Cinema is Jack Ellis and the Manager of the Capital Cinema is Charlie Twible, both pals of my father, to whom they give free passes. In addition to owning a cinema, Jack Ellis also sells furniture. Jack Ellis is a Jew.

Wally and I see 'The Wizard of Oz' at the Grafton and then 'The Thief of Bagdad' (with Sabu) at the Capital on the same day. Going home in the bus I am sick three times.

My father buys cartons of cigarettes from Dermot Morris, my father's solicitor who also runs a tobacconist's shop near the Moira Hotel. The Moira Hotel has a grand smell. My father orders tea. The waiter calls him 'Mr Ruttle'. Dermot Morris orders a ball of malt. 'Walter, Daniel,' my father

74

says, 'my sons'.

'Grand lads', Dermot Morris says, 'I only hope they grow up to be like their father.'

Dermot Morris played full-back for Ireland.

At Lansdowne Road my father points out to us a small man walking below the stand, carrying a grip for his boots and togs. 'The famous Con Murphy,' my father says. 'Neither man nor ball can pass him.' Con Murphy walks towards the changing-rooms.

Dublin girls wear frocks so thin that you can see right through them. It's spring. The crowd is roaring. My father draws our attention to George Morgan. He moves like a ghost from the base of the scrum, throwing himself full length, the ball curving from his hands, no one can lay a hand on him, as a line of blacks and whites move against an advancing line of pale blues, and the crowd chants 'Rock, Rock, Rock!' It's my father's old college. He ran and won against de Valera in the 880 yards. 'A bloody hill-and-dale ruffian,' my father says, 'with blood on his hands.'

Sometimes, for variety, we go to the Holy Cross Church in High Street, again among the last to arrive and among the first to go, indifferent Catholics who never get beyond the porch. I hear bells and coughing inside and my father, sighing, kneels on his handkerchief.

A stern Dominican calls out from the pulpit, interrupting his sermon to address the men standing at the back, telling them that there is room inside the church. The men shuffle their feet and advance on tip-toe into the church, holding their hats. My father stands his ground, staring bleakly ahead as if he had heard nothing. We hear the raised voice of the Dominican within, addressing those men still standing at the back, who were deliberately putting themselves beyond the reach of the word of God, whether this was their intention or not, now the voice coming closer and the tones more acid. Was that their intention? the voice asked. He was standing in the middle of the church, the congregation were all staring back.

'Yes, you and you and you standing back there,' the voice says. This was God's house and He came down to be amongst us at the Consecration. Were they too ashamed to come into God's house? Feeling acutely uncomfortable, I stand beside Wally. At breakfast my father repeats what the Dominican had said.

'Hadn't he a hell of a neck to go and say a thing like that?' my father asks, striking the edge of the table with his knuckles for greater emphasis. 'Hadn't he now?'

Whereas I had been afraid that the furious Dominican would appear among those standing at the back, force us into the church or expell us from it. My father threatens never to darken the church door again. My mother says nothing. She has a pious wish that one of her sons might discover a vocation for the priesthood. My father, rising and folding his napkin, says that he was 'stunned' by the impertinence of the visiting Dominican.

'Savanarola how are you!'

I take a bundle of English newspapers into the rockery to study the long sinful legs of the variety girls in the *Sunday Dispatch*. The tennis court is cut and rolled, the white guide-lines straight and true. Pulpy red berries fall from the yew tree, I smell freshly watered roses. I think of the Sunday dinner, the Bowsy's prime roast served up with flowery potatoes and fresh peas. Jelly and Bird's Eye custard. In the study of Nullamore I come upon an illustrated book called 'Paris Salons, Cafés and Cabarets.' A monochrome nude woman poses in a shadowy studio.

CHAPTER XI

In the Forbidden Places

I

THE HAND & FLOWER PRESS

I become familiar with a photo-girl in a field of wheat, crawling naked between the stalks, carrying her (and others, like her, also naked) in my hand. She is my first real naked girl.

We never speak. She is a London photographic model, nameless, standing without a stitch, with rising wheat up to her behind. She is half-turned away. I abuse her in the wheat.

Nothing can ever change or disturb her. She is perfect, naked and coolly regarding me. Her expression does not change. She watches me.

I strip and sink into the cold water of the cattle trough. When the cow-men water the herd they fill it. Green moss, brown at the roots, slimy as seaweed, covers the interior. Total immersion excites me. I feel so strange that I do not know myself, push into the mossy bed.

A gap, at first quite narrow, opens, widens for me. I press against the sides of the moss, streaming away from the sides. As I move deeper the tank overflows.

Curious young polly bulls and heifers come to stare at me with big clouded eyes over the broken wall. Their eyes are mauve and violet like oil on water, their hindquarters caked with dried dung. They move, scratch their throats on the wall, roll their eyes, suspicious of what I—all atremble now—am up to in their water. I hear a roaring in my ears like the ocean.

It begins to rain. Needles of rain touch and sting all

around me on the water. It's best in the rain, then my solitude is complete. I push deep into the moss, hardly knowing what I am doing. What floats out of me resembles frogspawn. I examine my ravelled tip and what has shrunken as the skin drew back. Have I injured myself?

Presently it begins all over again—elevation, push, contact, deeper push, tumult, frogspawn. I take it in my hand, taste it in my mouth. The heifers and black polly bulls observe me with their violet-and-mauve eyes, butting each other, shitting while watching. I climb drained and enfeebled out of my Roman bath.

I see tatters of shifts in the shrubbery over the wishing-well. I bend, drink mineral-pure cold water that pulses from an underground stream. The lads kick football below the hill where girls are running downhill, screeching.

In the plantation, among the leaves, in the fields, close to the ditch, I come upon soft outdoor stools, unmistakably she-shite, and wonder who deposited them.

'With yourself or with others?' the priest murmurs. I see a tilted profile against the grille. He does not look at me. The nun tells us that the secrets of the Confessional are sacred, and in any case always forgotten by the Confessor as soon as he leaves the Confession box. I smell the wood.

'With myself, Father,' I whisper back.

The face comes closer to me; the voice tells me not to let this sin catch hold of me, for it would lead to more serious mortal sin. He gives me a penance. Three Our Fathers and a Credo. 'Do I know the Credo?'

'Yes, Father,' I answer in a low voice, hearing the people stirring in the church, thinking how I will burn a candle. I hear pennies dropping into the box.

'Go in peace now my child,' the priest murmurs. 'Say a prayer for me.' The little judas slides shut.

Seated in the stern-sheets of an oarless boat chained to a tree, I stare into the Garavogue. My sinful face stares back

78

at me. Little fish, minnows and gudgeon mixed with perch and small trout, move anonymous as a dream under the chained boat that rocks a little as I move, bending over to peer down into the depths. I am dreaming of my great trouble that comes in the attractive shape of Hazel Ward.

Bask in the dream.

I am naked now, curved about the boat. The river embraces me. The rounded hull is slippery. I come up awkwardly against the swelling female-shaped underpart. Toothless sucking fish touch me, scores of them attack my yellowish sunken body. Far down in the depths the devils laugh.

Weakened and barely holding on, I see something move on the far bank among the bushes—a vixen come down for water? Hiding her face and blushes, clutching clothes she has just removed, Hazel Ward stands there. I pray for her to drop her clothes; she does so, comes naked to the river, begins to swim towards me. Hidden behind the boat, I hold onto the chain below the hull where I have written with a wet finger in code: 'Lezah Draw I adore thee.' Her face appears alongside the prow of the rocking boat.

Hazel Ward walks fully clothed on a path covered in moss. An abstracted girl innocent of guile saunters there on Protestant land, out of bounds for me.

Meanwhile, with a fine impartiality, I scatter my seed in loft and barn, outhouse and tool-shed, into grain and wet grass, dry leaves and river sand, in the woods and in bed, but mostly and with keenest pleasure under water. The polly bulls hardly bother to stare at me, sunken in their water, I come so often. So I set up my Hand & Flower Press, devoted solely to self-abuse, there in Sligo, in the long ago.

I slide feet first into the tepid brown water in the ditch, a soft collar about my neck. I see reflections of leaves and flowering hawthorne in the stream. Russet-coloured heifers with white chests graze in the field with two race-horses.

The heifers come down to the ditch to drink and discover me submerged. Long slobbers of saliva hang from their working jaws. Chewing and ruminating they watch me. I slide long and deep into brown profounder, my mind empty of images, nakedness and total immersion being sufficient stimulation. Discoloured water the temperature of blood holds me in a loose grasp. I sink into hot mud. The roaring in my ears is the circulation of hot blood, I smell fresh trampled grass, liquid cow manure, the shock and repeated shiver of contact goes through me and I am one with the animals shitting and shameless. Fibrous stuff floats out of me. I see my face reflected in the water. Creeping from the ditch I dry myself with a pocket handkerchief and dress near a bed of nettles.

2
THE SEED BULL PETER

Wally and I stand on a damp haycock and wave a red cloth at the heavy old bull who stands up to his knees in aftergrass. A short-tempered beast with little bad-tempered eyes, bloodshot, and all his weight gone forward, 280 sons gone out of him, Peter is no longer dangerous, but moody, to be avoided, standing by himself in wet aftergrass.

We wave and shout at him, but he does not stir or show that he has seen us. Then, when we have given up all hope of disturbing him, he looks up, fixes his terrible red eyes on us, two fools waving from a haycock that is already subsiding, and comes lumbering across, heavy as a tank. We leap from the haycock as it collapses and run for our lives.

3
THE STALLION

And now trembling as if entering into the presence of what is sacred, summoned by a surreptitious joy, I am preparing, undressing by the lake. I lie in it. A roan stallion in the field above prepares to mount the bay mare. They are preparing to do it, their eyes wild, nostrils opening and closing like bellows, kissing and biting in the mane of hair, the big teeth taking now hair, now hide. Hair falls across the mare's whitened eyes as she fans her tail. Now the stallion is on his hind legs, his hooves above the mare's back, and what he has extended is six times longer than the longest ever seen, four times thicker and twelve times heavier than my own poor thing which hangs between my narrow shanks and frequently causes me much grief. He goes trembling in his haunches, and under the lifted fan of tail the dark thing has gone right in.

Stretching along the mare's back, thrust under the lifted tail, the stallion pushes; they dance forward, haunches trembling, the mare bearing the stallion. I see the bay's haunches take the shock of repeated impact that goes like a wave along her broad substantial back.

The strike is dangerous-looking and occurs high off the ground.

I watch from the lake, the water up to my chin, floating. There are the two of them, a fierce claiming, two eagles with half-folded wings struggling over the grass. I expect to see blood. Instead my pathetic offering floats up.

Flowering puberty.

4
THE VICIOUS BITE

I crawl into the wheatfield. Lying naked, prone on a large pocket handkerchief, I copulate with a ghost-girl. Five comings are not unusual in daily sessions. I wash the handkerchief at the trough. Carry it rolled up and damp.

The Hand & Flower Press is set up. I work it hard. In out-of-the-way places such as deserted barns, in the granary, while hanging from beams, in deserted cow-sheds, open fields, sunken ditches. Where fancy pulls. The Hand & Flower Press! The Hand & Flower Press!

Pulling back his skin, Cox directs a thin stream of piss through the high slit-window of the toilets and as it falls we hear the big girls screaming in the Ursuline yard. Coffey crouches above the door of the jax and lets it go between his legs. The stench is of ammonia and beasts, stronger than the reek of the lion house in the Dublin Zoo.

A heavy stick marks my hand.

My father, standing above me, pulls the window up, crushing the top joint of my finger as he releases it. I taste salt tears, and wonder has he broken my finger. The window came down on it. I eat scraps of bread and Bovril, watch the light fade over Ben Bulben. The tears dry on my face, my mother comforts me. Wally, his fingers in his mouth, watches from the door.

The laburnum bush is burning. Incandescent yellow blooms are spilling over the wall. My mother wears a demi-veil and white buttoned boots. I observe her smiling eyes behind the veil.

I cultivate a taste for meditation and day-dreaming. The pleasures that we derive from water and earth are something that continues from the far side of a vegetable garden and an orchard. The countryside touches me and excites. I am alone with her. Removing my clothes I stand among the trees, trembling. There are days when I think that all life is a game played beneath the sun.

Wally strikes me with a cricket stump and runs weeping into the house. Staggering in, I am punished for making him cry.

I walk into Slish Wood, find rings of pigeon feathers, rabbit droppings, the stench of a passing fox. It's an aimless kind of life that I lead and it seems that the thirst for what I wanted would never be satisfied.

I hide under the long table in the dining-room. The linen

table-cloth reaches to the floor. My father's trousers and my mother's skirt and Wally's bare legs appear. Growling in my throat like a mad dog I sink my fangs into the white calf of Wally's leg. He rises straight up with a high-pitched scream. I taste pure venom in my mouth. Wally staggers from the room.

'Come out!' my father says. My mother holds a napkin to her face. This time I have gone too far.

We stand against the convent wall for a spelling test and right in the middle of the test Wally faints.

My father and mother discuss the matter and decide that neither Wally nor I will continue with the National School. We will go to boarding school instead, Killashee.

Killashee is in Co. Kildare. La Santé Union, Boarding-School. We will begin to learn Latin, for College.

CHAPTER XII

The Thwarts

Seated in the moored and oarless boat I stare vacantly into the Garavogue, without design or purpose in my life. Gudgeon move aimless as a dream against the side of the boat where my hand hangs as if lifeless in the water. Thickened by the chill of the river, the hand that trails in the water hardly belongs to me.

I take it out. Freckled at the back, hairless, it's my hand alright. A marine odour clings to the fingertips. I put it back into the Garavogue. The day seems without end. The moored boat fidgets in the current. I stare down into the river.

The days pass.

I cycle about Sligo in an aimless manner, moving silently through the little plundered town. A real ladies-man is waiting by the corner of the Cease-to-do-Evil. A stunner approaches, dressed in a green two-piece. It's to me she hurries, it's me she embraces, I who am so uneasy in the presence of disturbing beauty, so easily put down.

'That Phelan girl needs the strap,' my father says, crossing his legs, drawing up his socks. He looks at my mother.

I hear splashing and cries in Lough Gill. Rain begins to fall. I creep between the trees. In the opening, down in the lake, I see two big schoolgirls bathing in the rain. I take off my clothes, watch them from behind the trees.

When the rain stops they come laughing out of the water. They dress and go cycling away, chattering all the time. The sun comes out. A haycock begins steaming.

The masher and the beauty in green walk away together, linking arms, laughing into each other's faces. I see her reddened lips, her powdered face.

'That Phelan girl is a proper hoor,' my father says at table. I look down at my plate, blushing to the roots of my hair. Pretending to have dropped a fork I bend down. The blood goes into my face. I see Lizzy Bolger's legs entering by the door. She carries a gravy boat, she is Rita Phelan's best friend. Rita calls out to her: 'I heerd you singing like a lark in there.'

The sister of Liam Meldon is called Angela. I study her legs at Mass. She has long black hair, wears high-heel shoes and has beautiful legs. Thinking of Meldon's sister's long black hair and her stylish legs I succeed in making myself perfectly miserable. She walks in a wet lane by the sea, alone, dressed in her Sunday finery. She attends the Mercy Convent at Ballina.

Grey geese assemble on the sands of Lissadell Bay. A plain late Georgian house stands there among woodlands darkening in the rain. I see dark grey granite. Clouds pile up over the house. A dog comes barking from the terrace, far away.

Lizzy Bolger gives me a Christmas present of a monkey on a swing. I smell her face-powder.

'Lizzy is the soul of generosity,' my mother says. At the Grafton Cinema Wally and I see Deanna Durbin in 'A Hundred Men and a Girl.' Lizzy sings 'Take a pair of sparkling eyes'.

Given to bouts of erratic piety, I carry a prayer-book about with me. It has a cover like horn or ivory and a purple bookmark. I kneel in prayer before a frog-infested pond. The frogs rise and sink with outstretched arms, kicking up powdery clay from the pond-bed. They sail up, jerking with their long hind legs, like skinny old bald-headed men. Kicking down, resolute, their gooseberry-coloured eyes narrowing, they burrow into the powdery clay, disappear. Tadpoles wriggle under the frogspawn.

Pollywiggles eat each other, working up from the tail. Sometimes three are stuck together, two of them eating, only the head of the first remaining, half the body of the second already gone. I see dogs and bitches stuck together. The lady-killer seems to be eating the face of the girl in green. A labourer with scummy lips discovers me kneeling before the frog-pond, my lips moving, eyes closed.

'A grand summer's day!' he calls out over the hedge. I pretend to be fishing. 'A lovely day,' I answer, hating the phrase, my false brightness.

Time passes. His red-faced brother discovers me in a less edifying posture, kneeling naked, poring over the *Lilliput* nudes.

'Twill be about the size of ye!' a hoarse amiable voice calls out in derision. I crawl behind a bush, watch him cross the field. He wears hobnail boots, is stripped to his waistcoat, carries his jacket and a blackened billy-can. I hear the cuckoo calling from the Crooked Meadow.

It has come to this. I must confess it all again. Confession is torment. The curate gives easy penance; the Parish Priest gives hard penance, wants to know everything.

I lean over the bridge wall. The river flows fast below me. I feel the wall vibrate. Two pretty cyclists pass. The river is full of fish. The town is full of pretty girls. The days are long. I see the shadows of the cyclists on the road. I can tell the time by the angles of the shadows. Fires glow at night all along Ben Bulben. The gorse is burning.

I walk by Lough Gill into a lost domain, advancing into a ferny region of sunken glens and small limestone hills. Hidden away there I remove my clothes.

How the air breathes, how inviting the secret places, how alluring the water! The girls go, the whole earth breathes, water invites, as I sink ever deeper into shame and abasement. My ways are devious. Closing my eyes I see Hazel Ward's skirt lifted, the thighs of Jenny Kearns, Angela Meldon's breasts, Pauline Squares's bare bum.

I see a film still of the French actress Vivienne Romance, walking in a street, naked under her fur coat. My mother will not translate 'Crime passionel'.

I float with the current that drags me down, pulling at myself, half drowning. *Atone!* the river murmurs. *Ochone!* The cathedral bells chime on the wind as I float on down, naked and empty. It is like a punishment, not a pleasure, to be repeated over and over.

Behind the fretted baize, in the wires and domed valves of wet and dry batteries that squeak and bubble, a young and seductive female voice says: 'Hello, we're going to play roley-poley today,' and is instantly cut off by howling static.

I go naked, roll in dry horse-dung, eat frogspawn, being taken with Jenny Kearns who has such gentle ways. Her hair is the colour of bracken, her name belongs to a hill. I imagine myself naked with her in the bracken. She resembles Evelyn Keyes, the Hollywood actress.

The roan stallion prepares to mount the bay mare who is awash with sweat. They are stuck together in a field of reeling hillocks. In a heatwave Wally squirts water over me from a garden hose. I pursue him across a field, over a ditch, and grimly into a wood. Wally runs before me, bleating. I have gone berserk. Overhead, in the coolness, branches meet. Dressed in a full length black bathing costume that hangs baggily down, I saunter through the wood.

A dart goes through the joint of my right thumb, hangs there biting like a rat. I hold up a cluster of feathers, a drop of blood. Wally runs crying.

My father appears before me with hand raised to strike.

Jenny Kearns sits on the parapet of the bridge, swinging her legs and watching me slyly. Her bike is propped up against the wall.

'Auld Nick is above on Cairns Hill,' Jenny Kearns says. 'He's watching us.' I look at her throat and lips; she has a lazy way of speaking. The devil in the hills, has he horns and cloven feet?

Jenny Kearns looks at me and laughs.

A brazen hussy at the cross-roads puts a thrawneen into my mouth and dares me to race her to the centre knot. 'I dar you and I double-dar you,' she says.

Her spluttering and constant tittering unnerves me. Her breath comes thick and fast. I see her approaching eyes, her working mouth; I bite the thrawneen short and give her best. It hangs from her mouth with my spittle on it. She intimidates me, is older than I; I do not wish to be kissed first by her, not by that loose mouth that speaks always of 'dances' and 'dates'. She makes as if to strike me on the face. Close to, I smell her. Her breath steams in the air.

'Take coward's blow!'

We stand face to face. She reaches out and touches my cheek. 'Gives a coort Danny.' She turns away, laughing again. For me she feels nothing but contempt. The frozen pump behind her is trussed up like a madman's trousers.

In the following week she goes with Grogan the groom into the hayshed. Grogan comes out half an hour later, looking pale. He and Rita Phelan begin going steady. Grogan, who can stretch cats, walks with Rita Phelan into Slish Wood. They disappear among the trees. I listen to the old sailor down on the Mall. In his youth, he tells me, he worked for the Pollexfens, shipped out of Liverpool, saw the world. Now he sits on the bollard. Grogan puts his hands on either side of my head, lifts me off the ground so that, cooley-eyed, I can 'see' Dublin.

Horses come galloping out of the top field. Valarian grows on a crumbling wall. The stiff wrought-iron gate creaks open and a stranger stands there, one hand in his trouser-pocket jingling small change. He asks for my Daddy.

Da stands in the orchard grass naked up to his waist, a knotted handkerchief about his neck, red as a beetroot, a finger pressed to his lips. He sinks out of sight again.

I tell the stranger that my father is nowhere to be found, and could he come again another day? (This is the

88

rigmarole my father has drummed into us: I-am-not-here. Tell-him-to-call-another-day.) The stranger stares at me in frank unbelief, extends a florin, takes his leave.

Evening falls.

Odour of horse and horse-manure. Grogan, whistling between his teeth, curry-combs the mare. He mounts a small foot-stool to reach her spine. A huge complacent eye observes me.

'She loves it,' Grogan says, combing, whistling tunelessly, pushing the bay flanks, feeling the hocks and tendons.

I see coils of steaming guts in a bucket.

Wearing leather gloves and smoking a Gold Flake my mother lays out quicklime. The plaster heron looks into the lily pond where the evening chorus of frogs have begun croaking. On the rockery path great glistening black slugs die. My mother lays out halves of orange peels. I hear swallows in the hayshed and Grogan behind the wall saying 'Whoa there me beauty' and the mare's hoofs on the ramp. My father walks in the garden with his hands in his pockets of his cut-down trousers. My mother remove dead slugs with a trowel. She wears gardening gloves, smokes Gold Flakes. My father watches her. I watch them from the henhouse roof which I have quickly reached from the pear tree near the tool-shed. My mother is pointing with the trowel at something my father bends to see.

I go for kindling into Slish Wood and come upon a pair of teal-blue knickers left at the scene of the crime. A hard fist holds my neck in a vice-like grip, presses my face close to excrement. It is something I must comprehend, something, after all, essential.

'Would-you-now . . . woodja nëow?'

'Would you fight your match?'

'Does your mother know you're out?'

'Gives a squeeze Danny,' a coaxy female voice says winningly.

The red-headed Cox is loosening his belt, releasing his braces, letting down his trousers as he squats quickly. The expression on his face suggests that he is going to burst. Hup-hup-hup-hup! Lowry Maher flogging the bar.

Brown river weeds stretch like long hair over the stones where small trout and perch hang against the current. Swallows come down to dip in the water, fly to the parapet.

'Dan-the-wran, the rix-sticks-Stan,' the rowdies chant, pointing in mockery (steam rising off the river). 'The-IMBA-cocktail, rimba-Dan!' The voices soar away in the odour of wood-smoke.

'Gives a squeeze!'

'Hubblebay!'

CHAPTER XIII

The Orrs of Carrick, Uncle Jack and the Whoopee

My mother went to a Finishing School in France. She can speak French. Parley-voo. Dilly Ruttle is her married name. Her maiden name was Daphne Orr. 'Dilly' is a pet-name. Reserved and shy, she was the youngest (and prettiest) of six sisters. The Orrs come from Carrick-on-Shannon, have a launch on the river and a brother, Aubrey, who shares digs in Dublin with Brinsley MacNamara who wrote 'The Valley of the Squinting Windows'.

Carrick means the weir of the marshy ridge—'Cara Droma Ruisg'. The Orrs travel on the Shannon down to Athlone, which is the centre of Ireland. And dead in the centre of Athlone stands Boucher's Boot Factory. My father plays golf at Rosses Point with Ben Boucher who is deaf as a post. He wears a hearing aid and has a posh English accent.

Uncle Jack Healy has a long nose and a fierce thirst for whiskey. He drives a Buick that pulls a caravan, travelling about with his wife Norah and their two daughters Honor and Maeve. In the morning, Uncle Jack's breath smells of whiskey. Never in his life, my mother tells me, has he done a stroke of work. He teaches me to suck eggs. Raw eggs are good for you. Athletes swallow them. Uncle Jack has been a sprint champion of Ireland. He smells of good clothes, tobacco, whiskey. I steal eggs from the back yard. You pierce them with a pin. Uncle Jack sucks in his cheeks. He has a brown face, blue eyes. His caravan and Buick are parked in the driveway. Maeve and Honor overrun Nullamore, Maeve in a scandalously short pleated white skirt. She climbs the railings, shows her legs. She is a tomboy. Her sister is more serious. They call my mother Aunty Daff. My father cranks up the gramophone, which plays 'Hold Your Hand Out You Naughty Boy'. Maeve Healy wears spectacles down on her nose, pulls terrible faces, then runs upstairs in an even shorter tennis skirt that exposes even more areas of white skin. My father and mother play doubles tournaments against the Healys, my father, red as rhubarb, wearing on his head a handkerchief knotted at four corners.

Uncle Jack, my father says, is a Gas Artist. He runs a speedboat called 'Whoopee'. Jack's as idle as the day is long, my mother says.

My father and mother pose for a commemorative wedding photograph, as 'bride' and 'bridegroom'. These are strange words: *Bride* and *groom*. Scarved and powdered, wearing white calf-length pigskin boots with many buttons, the bride carries a folded parasol.

The groom shows a pair of manly calves in checkered woollen stockings under plus-fours cut in the generous baggy style made popular by Bobby Jones. A tight-fitted checked tweed suit, a bow tie set at a rakish angle, a small curly-brim derby on the crown of his head, makes up the outfit.

They stand by the Hillman-Coatelen; its hood is lowered and a large trunk strapped into the rumble-seat. The travelling trunk is as commodius as a good-sized wardrobe. On the top and sides, painted in white capital letters:

MR & MRS D. J. T. RUTTLE
NULLAMORE, SLIGO.

The groom's foot is already on the running-board and his hand on the little door in the very act of opening it for the bride, as the camera shutter fell. A spare tin of petrol is strapped onto the running-board. The crankshaft hangs ready between the front wheels. 'I'll give her a dart,' my father would say. 'I'll give her a few darts.' He drives with wonderful incompetence, as ignorant of the mechanical workings as he is of the workings of his own interior. I am not yet born. Wally is seven years unborn. They are motoring to Mulranny. Ahead of them lie seven anxious barren years. Uncle Jack, wearing a safety-jacket, with his short hair standing straight up, drives the 'Whoopee' above the waves of the Shannon.

The river is navigable for six miles above the town, as far as Battlebridge. Grandmother Nelly Orr dresses in brown, a long skirt down to her boots, a white blouse with a black ribbon about her throat. She waits for the tardy arrivals. Wally and his brother. She walks in Jamestown garden, through Summer Hill, the Priest's Lane, as far as Battlebridge, posts a letter addressed to Mrs D. J. T. Ruttle, Nullamore, Sligo.

Sligo!—site of the old Jacobite wars, Roosky and the O'Sullivan Beare, the terrible winter of 1602. (A hero who was carried into battle on a litter and died in the hour of victory from old wounds!)

Wally is to inherit my mother's hazel-green eyes, her troubled and secretive nature, her morbid shyness. She reads, voraciously. When Wally and I are old enough, she will read to us on a rug spread on the tennis court, shaded by the old yew tree.

Meanwhile, with 'Whoopee's' throttle (and his own mouth) wide open, Uncle Jack skids over pewter-coloured waves.

The library at Nullamore dates from the previous owner's occupancy; hers is a name I will hear all my life: Mrs Warren. A dead dog floats down a moonlit river. My mother loves 'Down the Garden Path', English Royalty, Anthony Eden, Noël Coward. Reading suits our secretive and evasive natures. I like to take a book behind the window curtains in the bedrooms, pull the curtains round me. I read 'Kocknegrow,' 'The Arches of the Years,' 'Teddy Lester's Schoolday,' 'Beau Geste,' 'Twenty Years a-Growing'.

Our fantasies are of benign or severe Heads, beaks, canings, midnight feasts in candle-lit dorms, cads and bounders, playing-fields and prefects, tuck-boxes and the town below.

The day of the big match dawns fine and clear but the

Lubber, aided by a rascally game-keeper, has tied Teddy Lester to the sails of a windmill. Togged out in collarless pink, Teddy Lester, the plucky standoff half, runs on his toes. Ito Nagao feeds from the base of the scrum, while Digby covers himself with glory in the rucks and mauls. Now I am hankering after a long-legged girl with caramel-coloured skin (from sunbathing in a red Jantzen costume a size too small for her) on Bundoran strand. She has come again with her father to the hotel on the golf links.

The summers are long and hot, smelling of mown grass, Nivea creme, with corncrakes *Kraak-kraaking* in the meadows and swallows going *Weedy-weedy-weede* on the roof of the Great Southern Hotel. My father drinks in the bar, plays golf on the links that surround the hotel.

The Atlantic breakers come rolling in and on the drenched red costume with its plunging backline, exposing a dimpled back that turns browner as summer procedes, and the salmon-shaped Jantzen-girl dives from the curve of her groin.

She wades in a rock-pool of swaying seaweed sheaths, waiting for me to make a move. Her name is Pauline Squires, her father a doctor, her mother dead. She is the only child of Dr Cyril Squires of Monkstown. His daughter has bluish-green veins behind her knees. She likes yachting. Monkstown is by the sea. My mother does not like her. 'A right conceited little Minx,' my mother says, pursing up her lips, the knitting needles flying.

Then comes September again with jellyfish floating in on the neap tides and Dr Cyril Squires and his daughter are returning to Monkstown. I find a glass fishing-float on the beach. There is a message for me in the glass, in the knots of greenish glass where air-bubbles have solidified. 'The seaweed keeps bubbles of air, for the larvae to breathe.'

Eau: Faiblesse devant les tentations.

Feebleness!

94

CHAPTER XIV

The One from Carney, the 0.22 Rifle

She smells of ferns.

The texture of her skin is glazed and clouded as if grey-blue smoke clouded her living skin, giving to it a down of dusk. My furtive eye falls to the bulge of her rounded thigh, to the blue-green tracery of fine veins at her wrist where the bare skin shows through the vee of her glove. She wears a lady's wristwatch, her blonde hair is cut short to shape her face. She is brown-skinned. The same veins throb on her temples.

I feel embarrassment sitting next to her. We do not speak. Of what would we speak? She is older than I by four or more years, is more assured in manner. She lives in Carney village on the road to Lissadell. I want to speak to her, appear easy with her, but how can I be easy when the centre of all my lewdest reveries is sitting next to me, breathing and transformed? Tongue-tied, I must look down, where my lowered eyes find her thighs, her bare arms, her handbag. Neat and compact as herself, the handbag rests on her lap.

I imagine a sort of counterfeit intimacy between us, an imaginary intimacy. She would not mind if I spoke to her, but is probably just as pleased that I do not. Her father is a steward and game-keeper for the Gore-Booths, with a cottage on the estate. The mystery of the word 'Demesne' and the lure of her clouded Protestant flesh are one and the same, being forbidden ground to me. No intimacy was possible between us; years and religion, social background, all prevented that. Sometimes I cycle on the Carney road, hoping to meet her; I do not meet her. Sometimes in summer I go swimming between the bridges, because once I thought I saw her, or someone like her, bathing far away with another girl under the trees.

But the summer passes. Two valuable gun-dogs are lost in the woods, drowned or poisoned. A young lad is drowned. I do not meet her. Summer goes. The time of frocks and bare skin. That goes. She cycles down the Carney road with vegetables in her carrier-basket. As she goes by a sense of evening mist accompanies her, and the pain, which I had scarcely felt at first, keeps on growing. We do not meet, and if we were to meet, we could not speak. Of what would we speak?

I fancy that I detect something venturesome in her withdrawn gaze. Her calmness unsettles me. I am unable to look at her. She sits by me, breathing, transformed. When she looks out of the window I turn away, look out, and see her reflection in the glass observing me with some amusement. When she walks she wears high-heeled shoes and her calves quiver, showing blue-green veins behind her knees. She wears nice clothes. Her name is Hazel Ward.

Hazel Ward is studying to be a nurse in Dublin.

Troubled by puberty, I sit beside this pretty trainee nurse, breathing in a ferny scent and a flesh and hair aroma stronger than any cosmetics. She has a Protestant complexion. The old frump who sits behind touches her shoulder. 'Is it Hazel?' Craning back, turned away from me, she tells the frump that she has bought stockings in the city, describing the mesh and size. At Garnett's she tells the frump.

I think of the word *Garnett's* and listen to the whisperings of the old frump. I had seen my mother lift her skirt, seen the mark of garters where they grip the thighs; but have never seen a young one lift her skirt, never kissed a girl. I wonder what it would be like to kiss a pretty Proddy. I see Hazel Ward's brown legs with her skirt raised. Kneeling before her to kiss those odorous thighs.

My mother's cheeks are soft and hairless and I taste face-powder when I kiss them. But to kiss a pretty ripe young one on the lips, never. Her olive Protestant skin troubles me. I think of her as The One.

I sit next to the window. Lights shine down the way and people with parcels wait beside dogs. I encounter her glance, a moist and disturbing look that sinks into me before I can look away. She looks up at her parcel from Garnett's.

The bus goes down the hill, shaking from side to side as if it might burst asunder. I hear dogs barking and the lights are closer. A hobbledehoy with flaming ears lifts down her parcel for her. She thanks him. The Burr bus has arrived in Sligo, its windows splashed with mud and grimy rain. I watch Hazel Ward through the dirty window. She has a neat feminine way of mounting her bicycle, thrusting herself forward on the pedals, then subsiding back onto the saddle. She cycles away.

At times I see her, or someone like her, travelling by pony and trap along the intersecting lanes and paths of the estate.

Unable to begin . . .

'Actually,' Wally says, using it as a hiatus to block up possibilities. 'Actually I didn't.' 'Actually I will.' He reads Dickens, having discovered Mrs Warren's set in an illustrated uniform edition in the library, white dust jackets with the titles in red. Wally speaks of Mr Pickwick, Quilp, Sykes.

I come upon an incomprehensible poem and quote it to him, hoping to dumbfound Wally.

The Heavenly Circuit; Berenice's Hair;
Tent-pole of Eden; the tent's drapery;
Symbolical glory of earth and air!

'I don't understand that, actually.'

The 'Pig' Menton bowls twisters at the nets, cranking his arm behind his back and looking from behind his left forearm. Wally, padded and gloved like Ponsford, puts up the shutters. I field. We play on the tennis court, bowling into the long net. My father watches from behind the net,

97

praising Wally's correctness. Wally pokes and pokes, with his collar up, tapping the popping-crease, lifting his bat.

I stand, dressed in white shorts and tennis shirt, sandals and no socks, my hair parted in the middle, I bowl at Wally. I bowl, thinking of Hazel Ward. The 'Pig' Menton hits a six over the garden wall into the rockery. My mother is in the greenhouse, clipping off white roses with the long-handled secateurs. The greenhouse smells of tomatoes and roses.

The paths go over the grass and under the branches laden down with horse-chestnut and sycamore bulbs, directing the rutted tracks of the hay-bogies in autumn and the heavy carts in winter. She lowers her head going under the low branches, stopping before a gate.

She reins in before the gate, walks the pony over the cattle-trap. When she mounts from the rear it tilts up, she drives it, not using a whip, hair blowing in her face.

I walk on scuffled gravel near high lime-stone walls impossible to scale and buy strawberries and rhubarb from ashen-faced Protestant gardeners who let me out by a lych-gate, watch me go. Hazel Ward belongs there in those enclosed and forbidden estates, behind estate walls twenty feet high. Tall gardeners walk soberly there, serve the Gore-Booths and the Gregories. In the orchard strange birds roost, jays imported from South America. The high garden walls are guarded by silence; that is her place too, she belongs there in the walled demesne. A Georgian house with doors wide open, French windows giving on the terrace, and there a table with a white cloth set for tea, empty basket chairs on the lawn. Nobody sits there; no stir or sign of life. A long white curtain blows out through the open window and a maid comes out to arrange something on the table. Sometimes in the wood on a long summer's day I hear the halooing of distant gardeners. This place, forbidden ground to me, is an annex to her charms. The pain keeps on growing.

She walks there on a mossy path by the river. She is one of them; her father serves rich land-owning Protestants. I walk on moss-covered green pathways by the river, hear it murmuring behind silver birches, come to a five-barred gate, survey the long nettle-infested field. I am sitting on a wall when she goes by, not letting on to have seen me, a young Catholic lad squatting on a wall where he has no right to be. As she goes by a sense of evening mist accompanies her. I watch her; a part of uncertain life goes with her. Half a mile away stands Lissadell, its French windows thrown wide open. The keepers are on the lookout for trespassers on the estate, being under strict instructions to drive the rough boys out of the woods.

We move in silence, Republican irregulars, and they too move silently between the trees, armed with shot-guns. I, who after all am a convent-reared boy, go with the rough lads and prefer to think of myself as one of them, play their games, fear what they fear, shit as they shit on the mossy sides of ditches, mitch from school, get the strap, steal apples from Nullamore orchard, my own orchard.

'Wood yer owl-fella mind, sy 'e kum 'an kotch-us?'

No, I lie, as much a failure with one party as with the other, accepted by neither the Careys nor the Wards, hardly by the Orrs, certainly not by Gore-Booths and Gregories.

'Tha-fella needs a gude puck on the gob for himself so he does!' red-headed Carey says furiously, and the gingery hair of his neck stands up like a ruff of a dog. I see a white chest and arms abulge with stringey muscle. A ring forms.

In winter I collect dry kindling from Slish wood and come upon discarded maroon knickers. I, who am so easily put down, always have this girl Hazel Ward on my mind. Is it I, the Garavogue dreamer? No; real life has not yet begun, my real life. On the last Sunday in July I walk in procession to the shrine at Tabernalt. In summer, deeply freckled, I swim in the lakes. My maternal grandmother Nelly Orr walks in the garden at 1 Wine Street. Fiercely corseted, she poses by a sundial. Nothing would ever get the better of that old disinterested gentlewoman. I walk in the garden at 1 Wine Street, listen to the drone of summer. My seed, plentiful as frogspawn, floats in the two and a half mile stretch of river between Lough Gill and the town. My seed searches for Hazel Ward.

When the big girls come screaming like snipe down the slope of the Urseline playground, I jump from behind an archway and am in the thick of them to snatch at thick brown hair, drag at pigtails. One screams into my face, I smell jam and milk, hair and hot excitement, it's infectious, I pull at pigtails, run away.

Rita puts a thrawneen in my mouth, takes the other end in hers and dares me to race her to the knob in the centre. The thrawneen with spittle on it hangs from her mouth.

'Ah, give us a coort Danny.'

Hazel Ward stands calmly before me. My father, who knows everybody in Sligo, speaks to her, treats her in a heavily gallant manner that embarrasses me. He makes up to pretty girls. How uncomfortable for me to hear him say that she is looking prettier every day, when is she going to qualify, and would she then consider marrying either one of his two useless sons! 'This is my youngest lad Dan,' he says, gesturing at me.

'Yes' (taking me in with her eyes), 'I know. He is very polite but never speaks to me.'

'He is shy,' my father says.

What could I do if Hazel Ward came sauntering towards me from under the trees, but turn away, and with a kind of grim earnestness give her the path. She comes and goes, sometimes with another girl, more often alone. I am too inhibited to approach her. Her father I know: he has promised to sell me a 0.22 rifle that he will not be using again. It is an old gun but it can still shoot straight. He used it to thin out rabbits and hares, squirrels.

In mid-winter I tell him I will have the money by the spring. I begin to save up for it. He will offer me 'a very fair price'.

I see Hazel Ward pumping water, carrying feed for the hens, slink back into the woods, hear distant shooting.

In the spring, when I had the price of the gun, I go to her house again. Perhaps she herself would answer the door? I arrive there in the evening when she might well be at home. Her mother comes to the door. I hear him moving about in the back room, coughing.

'He isn't in.'

'I've called about a gun.'

'He's not at home.'

He appears behind her with his shirt open, his braces down, a shaving stick in his hand.

I show him the money, made up of florins and ten shilling notes.

'I'm afraid not, sonny.'

He gives a laugh, or what passes for a laugh among Protestant game-keepers, sober men; did he take me for a fool? The gun isn't his to sell, he tells me now. He stands lathering his face and watching me go. I do not encounter his daughter. What could you expect from the daughter of such a bare-faced liar?

CHAPTER XV

The End of Innocence

Little by little, day by day, the years go by, until they are all gone, used up, and my childhood is over, with the things of childhood. Jack Horner and Jack Spratt, Jack and the Beanstalk and Goliath, Goldilocks and Rapunzel, Dick Whittington and his cat, Puss in Boots, Noah and the Ark, the paired creatures and the Deluge, the Russian sleigh and the famished wolves, Teddy Lester and the bullying Lubber, as well as the hair stiffener and the subterranean toilets of the Grafton Cinema, the two boxers sparring and hissing between their teeth in the ring of the Town Hall, their oiled white muscles, the bigness of their boxing-gloves as they mime punches striking home. The dying goldfish in the cloudy bowl, a dead rabbit in a snare set by me, the lifeless goldfish with its entrails out, hanging head-down.

II

The pictures of the will are not to be compared with those of the dream, of the drifting brain. The former have neither the solidarity nor the beauty of the others.

Yves Berger: *The Garden*

C'est ainsi que je fons et eschape à moi
('Thus do I dissolve and take leave of myself')

Michel de Montaigne

CHAPTER XVI

Killashee

Wally and I were dispatched to a private preparatory school in the country. The prospectus came.

LA SANTÉ UNION CONVENT
OUR LADY'S BOWER
KILLASHEE, NAAS
CO. KILDARE

Subjects taught as prescribed by the revised Primary School Syllabus.

Special Facilities for P.E.

Pension . . . £21 per term

Laundry & Drill . . . £2 per term

Optional subjects: Piano, Riding.

CLOTHES LIST AND UNIFORM

(All Uniforms supplied by 'Our Boys', 24 Wicklow Street Dublin).

2 Dark Grey Suits, 1 extra pants.

4 Shirts—2 grey and 2 white.

2 Grey Pullovers—V neck (long sleeves).

3 pairs Pyjamas.

3 pairs White Socks.

3 pairs Grey Stockings.

12 Handkerchiefs.

3 Hand Towels.

1 Bath Towel.

1 Laundry Bag.

Dressing Gown, Slippers, Toilet Requisites, Clothes Brush,

Shoe Cleaning Materials.

1 pair Walking Shoes, 1 pair Light Indoor Shoes (black, laced) 1 pair Brown Sandals, 1 pair Wellingtons.

1 pair Blankets, 3 pairs Sheets, 3 Pillow Cases, Rug or Eiderdown, 3 Table Napkins.

Breakfast Knife and Silver Fork, Silver Dessert and Tea Spoons (All engraved with pupil's initials).

All articles of clothing to be marked with pupil's name and, in addition, the number '26' on articles for the laundry.

SCHOOL TIES, CAPS AND OVERCOATS ARE OBTAINABLE ONLY AT 'OUR BOYS'.

FOOTBALL: Green Jersey, White Togs, Green and White Socks,

DRILL: All White—Woollen Jersey, Twill Pants (short). Drill shoes.

Books and Stationery according to standard.

Fees to be paid in advance.

A Term's Fee is required previous to removal of the pupil in lieu of Term's Notice.

P.E. Instructor: Mr O'Neill.

Wally and I were fitted out. Father drove us to the boarding-school. We were to be in a class with Pat Rogers, John Quirke, Jim Morris, Cormac Brady, Liam Lynch, Hugo Merrins, Eugene McCabe, John Glynn, Eric Sanderson, Tony Sweeney, David Hogan, Peter and Aiken Austin, Ted Little, Jimmy Donnelly, Michael Cuddy, Pat Pullen, Frank and Joe O'Reilly, Pat and John Markey.

The Staff consisted of Madame Loyola, Madame Patrick Clare, Madame Ita Magdalen. The Mother Superior was Mother Mulcahy. Visiting days were on Sunday. Mother Mulcahy told our mother not to call for a fortnight, to allow Wally and I to settle in.

The Christmas vacation seemed very far away. Nullamore seemed remote: a small beloved spot by the Atlantic. Would we ever get home again?

I write 'L.D.S.' on the top page of my lined theme book. It means *Laus Deo Semper*, praise God always. When the page is full I will write at the foot. 'A.M.D.G.', which is Latin for the greater glory of God. So that all my work, full of errors, is in His honour. I see Knocknarae in the evening light, hear the cranking levers of the hay bogies, the *dills-dills* (Wally's childish name for them), and Billy Prendergast driving up the front avenue in his low-slung Riley. I miss Nullamore. I think: The place that never changes.

Are ye with me now avic? Are ye for me or against me now? Do ye follow me now? Haffner's peppery sausages bursting open on the pan, my father undoing his napkin. Killashee is cold, the smells make me feel uncomfortable, the nuns.

'L.S.U.' my father says to Tommy Flynn. 'Long suffering youths.' They lean together over the open tank. Yew berries float on the surface, tadpoles rise and sink, wiggling their tails. It's vacation. Nullamore seems to have shrunk. I read Conan Doyle. A fire burns in the nursery, my mother is in bed there, reading. My father brings the car to the door. Our trunks are packed.

We go down hundreds of steps into the sunken Pleasure Grounds, Madame's pets walking with her. I see the green dome disappear. A goldfish big as a cod hides under the lilies of the pond. Walking backwards and staring at the green dome, Glynn falls with a cry into the fish-pond. He wears bands on his teeth. Madame Loyola gives him a special exercise book to write his stories in. He writes of knights, Crusaders, ancient times. He writes: 'I was forestalled . . .' I see a jackass looking over a gate. We wear coarse jersies of sackcloth on play-up days. Our faces turn strange colours. We run in the thick grass. I score 200 goals in the Easter term. Wally wears a loose cardigan of greengage and candy with the stitching gone here and there. He knots his school tie, laces his boots. Wally is developing grand airs, I am developing sores on my lips and ankles. I read 'The Giant Mole'. Everybody is reading 'The Giant Mole'. I become unpopular ('I suppose he calls *that* a tackle,' Cormac Brady says). I hear of Eck, Hus, Zwingli, Euclid, the Diet of Worms. We walk the corridors in silence, it's punishment for the whole school. Madame's pets inform on us. She takes out the stick, sucks in her teeth, getting white in the face. Speaking is forbidden at lunch and supper, we go to bed in daylight. In Madame's classroom a reign of terror begins. I stand at the classroom door, then just outside it, am sent into the dark cubbyhole where the mops and brooms are kept.

'If I have to spend all day,' Madame says, 'if I have to spend all week, you'll get this right.' I am struck on the back of the head with a ruler. I hear the swish in the air, I feel the pain in my head, I cannot remember French verbs. Anthony Scarisbrick shows us the veins of his wrists discoloured and enlarged. 'It's not right,' he says.

'No surrender!' Louis Noonan cries.

Wednesday night is bath-night. We wear full-length bathing costumes in the bath. You must not lock the door. Madame Loyola shows us how to soap ourselves and cover up. Sometimes she empties a bucket of cold water over the bathers, rushing in. Madame Ita Magdalen comes from County Clare. She has herbivorous buck teeth, mad blue eyes and a foul temper. She will kill you if you do not know your French verbs.

Platters of thickly buttered bread are set out on the refectory tables. The light shines on the glasses. I can see the trees in the Pleasure Grounds. When the Refectory Sister forgets to put out dry bread and jam for me I go hungry to bed, being too timid to ask. I eat toothpaste, drink cups of water in the dormitory. It's still light outside. I see the fields of Kildare. I lick the paint off toy lead soldiers and hope to die. Always hungry, I develop sores that turn septic, the nun says I must wear gloves in class. It's a stigma. I pick at my face. Always hungry, cast down in spirit, lob-sided with misery, I am Captain of Cricket and football but generally last in class, except for Art and English. I am the best in the school at Art. Wally gets First and Second cards in subjects that interest him. He is requested not to sing in choir. Wally's singing puts the others off.

We play handball. Boys climbing above the ball-alley causes plaster to fall from Fr. McCarron's ceiling. It lands on him in the bath. I try to imagine the fat red priest in the bath with plaster from the ceiling stuck to his head. He hears our confessions and the nuns' confessions. A visiting priest asks us to box in the classroom. We pull the desks back and bring out the boxing gloves. The visiting priest asks Reverend Mother for a half-day. Basil Fogarty reads 'Hiawatha'. Hal Hosty sings 'South of the Border'. Bending low the stout priest strikes his breast and says In principeo erat verbum, et verbum erat apud Deum. We sing Veni Creator.

Wally gets poor marks at mathematics. Mine are worse. Wally is sick every term. He misses classes. Mother Superior looks like Eugene Pacelli. She comes every Friday to read reports and give out class cards. For Art first, for mathematics last. Madame Loyola beats us. We are hidden away in Killashee. A wearisome time begins. It has no end. The term engulfs us. We sing:

This time ten weeks where shall we be?
Outside the gates of miseree.
No more Latin, no more French,
No more sitting on a hard old bench;
Kick up tables, kick up chairs,
Kick old Mother Genosofee down the stairs.

Ten weeks. An eternity!

Always, always the Litany of Loreto, the nuns chanting behind us in the chapel, the long windows overlooking the garden, the goldfish-pond, a vista of trees, the odour of sanctity.

Always, always intervening, the odour of my mother's fur coats, the calling of the cuckoo in the Crooked Meadow.

College meant compulsory everything: class, gym, play-up, endless chapel, endless study, four years of Grammar, Syntax, Poetry and Rhetoric. Wire-pulling (in our dreams we would never become sated). The cleaning-girls were all hideous. In a cutting wind, members of the Sodality distributed raw meat to the poor. Sowing. Spooning. Horn. Dirty doggerel must be recited with sparkling eyes:

> The long and thin go far in,
> But do not suit the lady;
> The short and thick do the trick,
> And manufacture baby.

CHAPTER XVII

Record of a Record

Wally recorded:
'Fifth Test, Oval, August 20, 22, 23, 1938.

England 1st Innings

L. Hutton c Hassett b O'Reilly	364
W. J. Edrich c Hassett b O'Reilly	12
M. Leyland run out	187
Mr. W. R. Hammond (Capt.) lbw b Fleetwood-Smith	59
E. Paynter lbw b O'Reilly	0
D. Compton b Waite	1
J. Hardstaff run out	169
A. Wood c and b Barnes	53
H. Verity not out	8
B 22, l-b 19, w 1, n-b 8	50

Seven wkts., dec.	903

Mr K. Farnes and W. E. Bowes did not bat.

Australia 1st Innings	*2nd Innings*
C. L. Badcock c Hardstaff b Barnes 0	—b Bowes 9
W. A. Brown c Hammond b Leyland 69	—c Edrich b Farnes . 15
S. J. McCabe c Edrich b Farnes 14	—c Wood b Farnes . . 2
A. L. Hassett c Compton b Edrich 42	—lbw b Bowes 10

S. Barnes b Bowes . . .41	lbw b Verity 33
B. A. Barnett c Wood	
b Bowes 2	b Farnes 46
M. G. Waite b Bowes . . 8	c Edrich b Verity . 33
W. J. O'Reilly c Wood	
b Bowes 0	not out 7
L. B. Fleetwood-Smith	
not out 16	c Leyland b Farnes . 0
D. G. Bradman (Capt.)	
absent hurt 0	absent hurt 0
J. H. Fingleton absent hurt 0	absent hurt 0
B 4, l-b 2, n-b 3 . 9	B 1
---	---
201	123

Umpires: F. Chester and F. Walden. England won by an innings and 579 runs. Hutton's Test record took 13 hours, 17 minutes.

HUTTON'S SCORING STROKES - **364** RUNS.

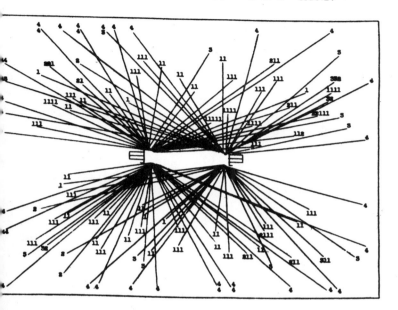

'The total of people who saw the game was 94,212, including 83,338 who paid for admission. The takings of £19,176 3s. od. are a record for a Test Match at the Oval.'

CHAPTER XVIII

The College, Its Secret Language

The Spiritual Father encouraged even *earlier* rising, not up at crack of dawn but in the dark, private prayers in chapel at 6.50 a.m., warning of a Godless world without, with its impure women waiting. 'My son,' Father Perrott whispered into my ear. A white figure passed into the distance, come from the Third Line changing-rooms. 'Looking shagged, Danno,' Owens my bad angel whispered. 'Little balls of fire.' His bitten finger pointed. Far away in the nets the loved one was sulking. Give or take, let all slide; all turned to impurities in the end. There were things done that never should have been done and vice versa, sins of omission, laziness. Reek of the locker-room, steam of the showers, narrow towels about narrow waists, brown waters of the Baths, blurred figures seen under the surface. The Line Prefect Father Kelly was everywhere, taking no chances. He had come from Australia. The 'girl' in the end-of-term play became the boy in the dormitory again.

'Soul of my Saviour,' I sang with the rest, feeling not pious but a perfect hypocrite, 'sanctify my breast.'

The wooden cleats of 'Dog's Hole's' rugger boots sounded like a chorus girl's high heels on the parquet flooring; his (her) abbreviated shorts was a lifted skirt; the stains suggested venery. An elbow dug into my ribs.

'Star in the east,' Owens whispered. He stared pointedly to where my fly-buttons were undone. 'Playing pocket-billiards again, old son? Tossing off again, eh?'

He could make his Wandering Willie stand up at will, a ferret stirring in a sack ('Bags first go!'). The General returned my geography theme-book unmarked. I'd misread one question. He sucked mints, a small embattled man chucking theme-books around Second Syntax. Owens 7 out of 10.

Ruttle, zero. Balls.

Fahy, small but furious, the legend ran, had fought a hated rival behind the Lower Line pavillion, both armed with hatchets.

Bob Tyrell played the French horn noisily in a deserted classroom, supine on the floor to escape detection and ridicule. Father Spike O'Donnell coached in the nets, took the House XV three-quarters. His rage was reputed to be ungovernable. His brilliant black hair was carefully parted. I made an extraordinary conversion.

The litany, the holy litany, the Little Treasury. An unbroken boy's voice singing and the hair of my scalp rising. 'Now my son,' whispered Father Perrott, 'what have you to confess to me?' On the inner door of a box in the Square a wit had scrawled: 'A man without a woman is like a fish without a bicycle.' An electric bell was ringing.

The tall Higher Liner Dagg thirsted secretly after Holland of the Lower Line who in turn pined for the exquisite soprano in the Third Line who sang a heartrending *Veni Creator*. The unbroken voice ascended, going up and up into icicles, blinding white clouds, rose-quartz, into nothing. My hair again stood on end.

Holding the wings of his soutane, Father 'Dog' McGlade climbed into the ornate pulpit, launched himself into another of his justly famous sea-Sermons. Combers were onrushing, gulls tossed, coasts threatened, mariners imperilled; the whole chapel shook. Holding onto the pulpit and leaning forward, as if on the poop-deck in a tempest, Father McGlade took the chapel by storm. He invoked wrath, wrack, spume, seawinds, monstrous tides; his never-feeble oratory rose to new heights of rhetorical-theatrical flourish and panache, arms wide, his hands clutching the pulpit, bringing down apocalyptic doom. The whole school, kneeling, was silent, drenched. Drenched by far-flung spume.

In the stinking gym, 'Handlebars' Hastings treated us to tirades, rashly insulted Roche, who lodged a complaint with the Rector. The public apology was no apology. 'A certain boy', Handlebars insinuated, twirling his waxed moustache.

Tossing, getting one's hole, 'offside' (the fart); unseen aloft behind us in the choir stalls the tenor Waldron sang *Stabat mater dolorosa, juxta crucem lachrimosa*: intractable amber. The clear soprano was Asphodel. *Never-return,* the voices sang, mingling. On a joyful wave-frequency the Latin seemed to come from afar.

At Sodality, in the private chapel, Father Ffrench made religion, piety, sound as safe, and dull, as botany. A small toad-like visiting priest, holding sterner vivisectionist views, made it sound dangerous as lobotomy. He put the wind up all his hearers. No love-notes were passed in chapel. The three-day Retreat wore on. Third Liners were excused these moral sermons ('spiffs'): Owens the Lower Line tack (a strict non-reader) did not engage in sticky piggyback with desirable Third Line sows and had no emission stains on his flies to cover with a book while leaving chapel with lowered eyes. The Confessionals were full. Spooning, sowing, making sheeps' eyes, bad thoughts and attendant acts were out. Father Perrott glided into the confession-box, clutching his soutane.

'Little gains, little losses,' intoned Father Ffrench. A voice of manifold reason. But other baser promptings might still prevail.

That time too was gone. The College. The long incarceration. The depths of the country. Self-abnegation and self-abuse. A bracing climate. Certain always-hinted-at-but-seldom-admitted-or-even-performed sexual irregularities.

There, moreover, another language was found, the little language of lovers with its capricious synonyms, adopted to lull suspicion, conceal obscure hankerings in the long ferment of two- and three-month isolation, away from all female company for terms at a stretch; not bog or dog Latin, some Greek mixed with old Gaelic, French, a little German, but a true secret language. The hours spent in religious duties had become an aphrodisiac—kneeling and standing, hymn-singing in May, the Third Liners with high and unbroken sopranos, the Lower Line contraltos and tenors, the Higher Line tenors, baritones and bass: 'Daily, Daily Sing to Mary.' Courtney and Bot O'Toole grining behind their Westminster Hymnals at Pierre Daly the tall house prefect in the first row of the Higher Line pews. They sang loudly 'Daly, Daly, Sing to Mary', watching the quiet wing-threequarter, the possessor of long spidery legs, and wondered about Mary. It might have been 'Roll Me Over in the Clover' or 'Eskimo Nell', they sang with such a fervour.

The secret language: box, to take a box, to book a box (to shit). The Square: the toilets, always guarded by the Gallery Prefect. Slash, slashing (to urinate). Spoon, spooning (court-ship). Sow, sowing (sodomy), as in Dut. *zog*. G. *sau*. L. *sus*. Gr. *hus, sus* (female pig). The toilets of the narrow boxes were often defaced, then white-washed, then defaced again. Barbed wire stretched above the high wall. Soliciting in chalk, was frowned upon, wiped out. At Declamation Fr. Kelly spoke of Pompeii's filthy walls. Many thousands of adolescent youths and young men had urinated against the slate. The college was old. Dog's Hole Burke went with The Black Sow into the locked games-room. Certain Lower Line 'tacks' (prefects-to-be) had dry bangs with Third Line sows in the deserted Lower Line library while the chapel filled for evening devotions. The assembled lines were long, stretch-ing back to the Baths. The chapel took three hundred with the Higher Line Prefect, Fr. Kelly, mounted behind on a rostrum. The Stations ended with a prayer for peace. Red-headed McGivern inscribed Fairy Moore's name in lovingly elaborate Gothic script in the fly-leaf of his Roman missal.

Love-notes came in curious forms in the college where

resistance was low, and whole forms dreamed of lovely boys, the bared thighs of those who had become girls overnight: the sows.

Shower-nights were electric with promise.

A glob of semen stuck fast to the wood of the box; as I watched it slid down. A naked male figure stood spread-eagled, with the testicles of a horse. A penknife had cut: 'T.O. loves B.F.'

I was never to enjoy the privileges and advantages of a university education, but went from college into an insurance office.

CHAPTER XIX

The Heavy Curtain

The study, or library, at Nullamore with the heavy curtain drawn and the door closed, two paraffin lamps lit and the wood fire burning, was hot as a furnace.

Wally, crouched forward on the edge of the commodious but uncomfortable smelly leather armchair, extended his hands to the blaze. Coal would give way to wood as trees were felled, and wetted slack give way to damp turf as the war dragged on.

Wally closed his fingers into a fist then opened them into a fan. A carpet slipper held the side door ajar.

The library, or study, was stuffy, smelling of coke, heated leather; a pot of tea and buttered toast warmed in the grate. Wally wore slippers: he was settled in for the evening. If a slipper was not jammed in the outer door it meant that golf practice was off ('Take a look at the back door and tell me if your brother's off golfing').

Wally made his way across the bleach-green with short rapid mincing steps, hips and shoulders agitated, an odd galvanised way of progressing; a limp canvas bag held a set of mis-matched hickory-shaft clubs. He played alone over the deserted outer nine, lifting his head, cutting great divots, hurling clubs about, cursing his Maker. *'Jeezus Christ!'*

Wally's golf was all practice, six or more practice swings followed by fresh-air shots, shanking followed by atrocious language. A distant misshapen figure with arms poised at the summit of a cranked rigid swing, stuck there, unable to get down. The slipper in the door prevented the door closing, a silent order that supper should be on the table at sundown when he returned, when Wally removed his spiked shoes in the porch and stepped into one slipper. Sometimes I saw him in the gloaming, pacing up and down in a drainage-ditch looking for a lost golf ball. His patience was phenominal.

The fire keeps subsiding. Wally poked at it, only stopping to stare fixedly at a stain on the tiles where milk had boiled over. For a nightcap he liked Ovaltine. He liked to stay up late. Sometimes he sniggered at the rapid-fire patter of Benny and Hope, cross-talk comedians, his rare laughter donkey-brayed far away, hee-haw, heehawing. My mother's rare laugh was high and hysterical.

Wally, warming the backs of his hands like my father, sighing, was not looking at me; if between us there was not silence, neither was there ease. Silence between kith and kin, between brothers, is common in Ireland; his solitary amusements were as sterile as his lonely sports, his incessant practice.

He had some theory about masticating his food, so many chews to the mouthful, moving his lower jaws in a lateral manner like a ruminant, a cow at the cud. Unnerving when he stopped chewing to glare. His hair had begun to fall out early, he would have a tonsure at thirty.

If he required anything at table, he cleared his throat twice *um-hum*, with a rising interrogative inflexion, and pointed with his chin to the salt, gravey, sugar. A double clearing of the throat followed or preceded by um-HUM meant May-I-have-your-attention-please; a treble *um-HUM* signified (testily) No-wrong-try-again. A pointed *Ah-HEM!* meant Cut-the-frivolity-if-you-please, or Don't-test-me-too-far. If attention could not be attracted by these means or if one flatly refused to look at him, Wally would be reduced to speech.

'*I say!*'

And then with elaborate courtesy, ask for whatever was required. But mostly he said nothing.

'What does he want, Dilly?'

My brother was retiring into silence. One fine day, as far as his immediate circle of relatives were concerned, communication was over. After that, nothing but grunts.

At college, as at prep school, the subjects that did not interest him (Irish, Mathematics, Science) he refused to study. Special rules had to be made for him; exempted from games and from punishment in a school that believed in both ('a good beating never hurt any boy'); under threat of punishment Wally fainted. Exposed to the drenched playing fields he caught pneumonia. When the echoing corridors resounded with the noise of the pandy-bat, Wally was safely tucked up in the infirmary.

And then, silence. His inexplicable black-out choler. During seven years' detention in two boarding-schools he had become withdrawn, reverting more and more to silence. In the family circle he was dumb, had become torpid, was putting on weight. Tennis was finished between us (Wally in flannels and head-band serving his extraordinary complicated service, calling out 'Duce!' 'Thirty-fiff!', disputing the score in a lather of sweat, retrieving high volleys from the orchard, the beech hedge). Now, alone, he bowled into the cricket net for hours at a stretch, aiming at a single stump. (The sun high and the shadows sharp, Voce comes in to bowl. A heavily-built man. He comes pounding in, propelling himself at the wicket. The batsman stabs at it, gets a thin inside edge, the ball squirts into the slips, where Hammond is waiting. Spectators applaud on the roof of Archbishop Tennyson's School). Pounding down the crease, aiming at a single stump, nothing seemed to discourage him. Every evening he walked by the beech hedge, wearing a path as polished as linoleum.

He had opened the batting for the College XI. Once dug in—and his innings was one long tireless process of digging in—he was difficult to remove. His refusal to take any chances inhibited scoring strokes, partners were run out, halfway down the pitch, Wally held up a batting-glove, Wait. No run!

His partner left, cursing him; but Wally was immune to

criticism and, scoring nothing, stayed there longer than most, sometimes through a whole innings, carrying his bat. He played a ghastly game of cricket, making his own rules, slowing it up to a dream-like pace; pads and peaked cap, his collar up, jabbing and poking, levelling the pitch with the back of his bat, picking up straws, studying the field placements. He kept records: the time spent at the wicket, questionable or 'wrong' decisions. The umpire and coach was Harrison of Notts, a former county player, a professional.

'Ruttle,' Harrison said, 'blimey, wot a blightah!'

W. J. B. Ruttle c. Hayden-Guest, b. Blood-Smith 12

Fr. Gerald O'Byrne told my father that he had no personal objection to the college XI playing against Protestant, Masonic or even Presbyterian schools, but that he (my father) must understand that all those with double-barrel names (Gifford-Clarke) were the illegitimate off-spring of English titled people. Fr. Gerald O'Byrne ('The Razz') took Wally for Greek; he was a classical Greek scholar, and had once fought an anti-Christ with his bare fists in Madrid. He disapproved of cricket, on principle.

Once he had identified a Republican corpse on a Spanish battle-field, projected on a screen, as a mountain range near Malaga. His soutane was chalk marked, he wore thick spectacles, he was considered brilliant.

Wally crouched at the edge of the crease, at the edge of the dream, tapping the white line, bracing himself. When finally removed he went walking very slowly back to the pavillion, removing his batting-gloves, ignoring the incoming batsman, walking towards the silent crowd as though a wrong had been done him.

At home in Nullamore now Wally lived his own life. His work-room stank pleasantly of turpentine and oil-paint. He was putting the finishing touches (the lettuce) to a meticulously accurate copy of Gainsborough's Boy with the Rabbit. As a copy it was fair, as a painting, dead.

He had arranged his life in a particular pattern and any deviation from it would be intolerable to him. Inflexible, torpid, silent, crouching close to the fire, he drew out a large pocket handkerchief, trumpeted loudly into it, folded it, put it away. He was given to heavy nose-bleeding. At school, I believe, he could bring this on at will, a positive splashing at the back of the class announcing that Ruttle was having another nose-bleed.

The wireless knob was within easy reach. The reception was poor, the batteries dying. Wally took hold of the woodwork, buffeting it, cursing it. He had heard war declared, came into the kitchen to say 'War's just been declared.' Old Mrs Henry blessed herself and said God help us all. The nagging jeering voice of Lord Haw-Haw came now from Berlin, jamming the BBC.

Wally confided to a small pocket diary and was forever making notes in a small neat hand, unaltered since his writing was formed. He refrained from using my Christian name and, on the rare occasions when he spoke to me, employed a coldly reserved deflective tone that killed any frankness or intimacy. His smile was thin and deprived, it put him apart. He studied his pale manicured hands, at them with file and buffer, orange sticks. He began to study Morse Code at Atlantic College in Dublin, taking a room in Mespil Road. He had volunteered for the Royal Air Force; night-fighters, above all things. My mother told me. 'That's what he wants, apparently,' she said. Wally was on the side of Gubby Allen and Bill Bowes, Jack Hobbs and Lord Burghley, Don Budge and Kay Stammers against Dr Goebbels and Julius Streicher, Alfred Rosenberg and von Ribbontrop ('*Only* a champagne salesman,' my mother said; she preferred Anthony Eden, who was a gentleman), Lili Marlene and Göring. He was waiting for his call-up papers.

He went to Cranwell cadet-school. On leave, he walked through blitzed London, in the black-out, between alerts. Pat Kirkwood stood on the stage showing off her wide smile and long legs, singing 'Oh Johnny, oh Johnny, how you can love!' He saw Terence Rattigan's 'Flare Path'. My mother loved royalty, and Wally loved England. Was this the same fellow who had listened to Yankee baseball games and American football, ice-hockey and basketball, the same with whom I played 'William Tell' in the orchard at Nullamore, shooting apples off each other's heads with a Daisy air-rifle, the same with whom I had played Tig ('You be *it*'), who had run on fat legs, crying, embraced a tree—'*Pax!*' The tangled branches of the apple tree fell across his face; it was the same. Göring splashed unseen on a private beach in Germany, the sign read VERBOTEN! Wally, among other cadets, officers-to-be, grew a moustache, studied night-fighting techniques. Wally as a child, shouted in a child's voice: 'Mafeking is relieved!'

I had not now for some years enjoyed much of his confidences; he had withdrawn into himself, kept his own counsel. Pared his nails.

CHAPTER XX

The Institution

Wally and I were sitting before the fire, not speaking. Nothing unusual in that, for now we never spoke to each other. One day he closed up and after that you could get nothing out of him but grunts.

He was sitting forward in his easy-chair, staring into a heaped-up fire of slack that burned in the grate. Behind him, on the table, cartridge paper had been tacked down and drawn on in one of his coldly perfect designs. T-squares and set squares, ruler and eraser, callipers and Indian ink, mapping pens and sharply pointed pencils cut down to a third, all meticulously set out. A pot of tea and buttered toast stood warming at his feet. He worked every evening after a day in the quantity surveyor's office; worked steadily and neatly for final examination, not tolerating in himself anything short of perfection, and flying into a great rage if his papers were shifted or disturbed in any way. Indications of displeasure were conveyed through his mother, who cooked for him, saw to his washing, mended his socks. His life was arranged in a set pattern from which any deviation would not be tolerated; life without order was intolerable to him. At home he spoke only to utter heartfelt curses, sucking the dear Redeemer's name out of the impalpable air . . . *'Jesus Christ!'*

Our father was a passive, evasive man who only wanted to agree with people, at least to their faces and mother deferred to him, in company at least; from where did this Corsican fury emanate?

On this particular evening he was not working, but sitting before the fire in his weekend pullover and carpet slippers, looking into the fire, sighing at intervals, looking at his hands. The fire spluttered, sending out licks of blue flame.

The thin smoke was drawn up the chimney, released into the darkness and blown away. A sudden green jet of gas spat out at right angles, aimed at Wally's ankles. Wally sat crouched as close as he could get, the pot of tea at his feet, the jar of home-made jam, the wireless knob within easy reach. He liked to work to subdued music: Sinatra singing 'Moonlight in Vermont'. Hoagy Carmichael's 'Stardust'.. 'Begin the Beguine'. His favourite programme was 'Hi, Gang!' Ben Lyons (a fatly unctuous voice) and Bebe Daniels, Vic Oliver, serenading the Marshall Plan in close harmony:

Gee, Mr Roozy-Felt, it's swell of you,
Thewayyou'rehelpingustowin-the-war!

Perhaps Wally was secretly in love with Bebe Daniels? Next to 'Hi, Gang!' he liked AFN broadcasts of American news and entertainment programmes, cross-talk between Jack Benny and Bob Hope, sports coverage of baseball and American football, ice-hockey. The fast wit sometimes drew a snigger from Wally. The wide-open vowels of the newscasters must have pleased him, assertively open: 'Nö-WOW' they said for now. 'OW-ër' for hour. From six until midnight he sat by the wireless, turned the dials; on wet weekends he monopolised the set. My father was disinterested, immersed in newspapers. My mother listened only to *Mrs Dale's Diary*.

But on this particular evening he neither worked nor tuned in to AFN to hear Sinatra singing about Vermont; other matters occupied his mind. Some uneasiness troubled him.

I had enjoyed a little of his confidence while we were in boarding school and later at college, but towards the end of his time there Wally had begun to withdraw into himself, to close up. He had no friends; he confided only to a small pocket diary, meticulous records of day-to-day activities, his sharp judgements on people. Never in his life had he used my Christian name; it was 'you', or *him*, or *that fellow*. Once it had been 'The Brat' (the bite under the table, the ill-judged snowball); never Dan. And to his father the same unwillingness to call him 'Da' or Father; the same foghorn voice mooing in the distance. Keep your distance. Stand off.

Wally was mean to my mother, even cruel, like a lover. Smirking, looking at his well-cared-for nails, having his own way, even sharing jokes.

'He has a lovely smile,' my mother liked to say. 'When he chooses to use it.'

It was a rare smile. When Wally brought it out, his brown eyes twinkled, his head wobbled, his lips curved and, shaking all over, Wally went 'Hehehe, hehehehe!'

'Piece of cake,' Wally said through compressed lips. Cole Porter's 'Night and Day'. Gershwin. The continuing war.

Now that he wanted to speak, he found it was too late; he could not. It was years since we had spoken to each other. Living in the same house, eating at the same table. We had accepted this as quite natural, if that was what he wanted; we would have accepted anything he did, no matter how unnatural. Wally growing corpulent, taking short womanly strides, that secrecy of his, the rare soprano giggle.

'Hear that?'

I looked over at him; had I heard aright, had he addressed me? He was fixed rigid on the edge of his chair, wringing his hands. His profile told me nothing. He looked as poised as the jumper on the high parapet. He would not look at me. Wally all his life, his adult life at least, had avoided exchanging eye-glances, hand-clasps. I strained my ears, waiting until he spoke again. He sat there rigid, his tea untouched. There was something in the air between us; faint as the singing of telegraph wires in the country, in the winter, far removed from human habitations. Some alarming or tragic message hummed in the wires, over frozen ditches; somewhere a hand, hesitating, reached out, lifted a receiver; an ear heard. I did not speak, leaning forward in the same pose as my brother. He would not look directly at me, only that oblique look he had for others. His attention appeared to be directed at a violet cone of coal gas that curled through the bars turning a vivid green as it emerged, fiercely ejecting a funnel of brilliant white smoke. It spat gas.

'Hear it?'

Silence, but for the gas. It fanned out, withdrew itself behind the bars again, subsided. Unconsumed slag, dry now, eaten with fire from within, fell into the heart of the fire. It was too hot. Our faces glowed.

'Hear what?' I asked.

Wally made an indistinct sound in his throat, heaved himself out of his chair as he pushed it back, hurried in an awkward way out of the room. He had taken the red-hot poker with him. I heard him scuffling out, heavy on his feet, the sound of the wooden bar being dragged from the back door; came a gust of cold air, and Wally vanished into the night.

I stayed where I was. After some time I heard the door being bolted. He came in and sat down again, replacing the poker. He was breathing hard, white in the face, sweating. I looked into the fire where the jet of gas had retreated back into the flames.

Then the pale hands were extended once more to the flames, to the toast, the knobs, to 'Moonlight in Vermont'.

One damp afternoon I visited Wally at the mental institution known as Hazelwood House at Ballina, taking the bus across in the rain to that low town. The prevailing wind was blowing in dirty weather from Killala Bay, the streets deserted save for a few miserable curs and cyclists. Ballina was awash in cowshit. Passing an open doorway through which came the odour of roast beef, I made my way to the institution and asked for my brother. I was informed that he was waiting for me in his room. He had a bad cold.

'Oh, hullo,' the faint voice said as though we were at

home. He seemed pleased to see me, and did not appear to be demented or altered in any obvious way; not until he spoke.

Wally spoke!

That was an event in itself. He had filled out; certainly they were not starving him. He looked quite bloated, and spoke in that far-away wind-voice he used so sparingly at home, asking for this and that at table, before subjecting what was placed before him to that microscopic study with which we had grown familiar, the long chewing process that followed. He spoke a lot, for Wally. Electroshock had changed him, had loosened his tongue. It was much like being back in prep school with him, all his hopes intact, going down the 360 steps to the sunken Pleasure Gardens, so-called, the swimming pool silted up with dead leaves. Madame Patrick Claire walking with her pets hand-in-hand.

My drenched raincoat was steaming on the radiator, the exposed rubber lining gave off an unpleasant odour. The room stank of Institution; it was like boarding school on the first day of term, the place full of new faces; only this was worse. I draped my sodden raincoat over the end of the bed.

'What do you know about snow?' Wally asked, nodding his head, half-smiling.

I was taken aback; what did this signify? Once I had thrown a snowball that had struck him about the knee, filling the turn-ups of his trousers. I stood in the ditch below; Wally looked down at me, a coldly dismissive stare. 'Take that out!' was all he said; and I had obeyed.

'It falls in winter,' I said lamely now, 'From the sky.'

'No.'

'No?' I said.

Wally made a canonical gesture with his hands.

'It comes up out of the ground.'

I looked at his pale hands, marked by hard manual work, those unused hands of his. Work on the land he must, the doctor had said, in order to be well again in his head; and we had believed him. We would have believed anything. Had the shock treatment addled his brains?

'Oh?' I said, watching a puddle form on the floor under my raincoat.

Wally pressed his hands together between his knees. He opened them to reveal discoloured bruises, calluses that had split.

'You find the work hard?'

'Yes,' Wally said, staring at his marked hands 'It is. I do.'

For years now we had not spoken or exchanged confidences, avoiding each other's eyes. It was possible to be in the same room and yet not acknowledge the presence of another. Wally now was even looking towards me with that humid brown eye. He did not seek to catch mine, but looked off to one side; it was close. He regarded me from the side of his musing eye.

Feeling ill at ease, I searched for subjects in my head, but could only think of the Hurley brothers, who lived in Ballina. What had become of the Hurley brothers? One had been in Wally's year, one in mine, both bettering themselves before entering their father's grocery trade; both had distinguished themselves at mathematics, my worst subject; one was known for his prurient ways, his filthy limericks. Two great oafs, scummy-lipped champions of the ruck, the brawl. They had come and gone.

'Where are the Hurley brothers now?'

'Here,' Wally said, his head wobbling. 'Both here. Poets.'

I looked out the window where a pack of grey clouds were being driven before the wind. A cold damp day at the end of a wet week in the latter end of a wet year. It was Sunday, visiting day; it felt like it. In college days, our father had called in a closed car; we drank Bulmer's cider, handled the clippings he had cut from newspapers, miscellaneous information, a pilot decapitated in Japan, Panzer divisions and pincer movements, maps of the war in Europe. Somewhere in the sodden town a dog barked, a church bell rang. What did I personally know of the ways of the world?

Snow, smelling like roast beef, rose up from the ground, the Hurley brothers putting their heads together, and farting loudly, wrote metrical poetry. Crocuses bloomed in cowdung in the depths of winter.

'No!' I cried.

'They spend the whole day admiring themselves in front of mirrors,' Wally said. 'They never go out.'

A dog was barking, a church bell ringing. My brother sat on the edge of his bed with shoulders bowed, pressing the palms of his hands together. At college he had fainted when about to receive 'pandies' (the leaded leather strap), had been excused punishment by Father Minister, wrote 'lines' instead, spending much of his time in the infirmary, well muffled up. Quick to pick up a virus; a model boy in all respects, no one bullied him. Others put on the gloves, wrestled on the mat, not Wally.

'Here in Hazelwood . . . Is that permitted?'

The Hurley brothers, scalped like convicts, gravely examining their faces all day in mirrors, opening wide their eyes, writing lines of poetry on small pads supplied by the Institution. Surely not.

'Yes,' Wally said with all solemnity. 'Here . . . downstairs.'

'Go to God!'

A knock on the door. Wally opened it. 'Tay,' a female voice said, and in came a slattern with a tray of tea and buttered bread. She set it down on a table by the window. A country-bred, convent-trained girl, often on her knees, close to subservience, smelling of Carbolic. There were two cups. The girl looked at the widening puddle from my raincoat, then at me, and went out. I poured. It was powerful tea. I handed a cup to Wally.

'You could trot mice on this,' I said. One of father's hoary witticisms.

I felt stupid; my thoughts were heavy and slothful. We spoke of relatives we had in common, a subject which did not interest me greatly; but Wally had always cultivated his relatives, an aunt in Adelaide, an uncle in the Argentine, Cissy Maxwell and the rest, all blood relations, unspeakable bores.

College friends too he mentioned, Wally who had no friends; he liked to keep in touch with the old Alma Mater, read the school annual, familiarising himself with the comings and goings and present whereabouts of former class-mates and teachers—Mike Clarson (maths), The General, Horney Ward (Science), Father Gerald O'Byrne (Ancient Greek). College is not a time I myself look back upon with any pleasure.

Wally assured me that he knew of this one and that and old so-and-so; all were known to him personally and were, furthermore, all downstairs, even the dead. Others too. All below Cousin McAllister killed under a tram.

I heard blurred voices calling in the corridor, heavy feet passing by the door. I thought of Wally working in the fields, going back passively with the others as daylight left the land, sitting at supper. Retiring early, too tired to think. Hazelwood House, the nut house. In the seventeenth century, the hazel had represented Stupidity. What did it represent today? Wally looking forward to visiting day.

I heard doors banging in the corridor and the sound of visitors leaving. Time was up. I gave Wally the parcel from his mother, knitted socks and a spare shirt, cake and newspapers. Somewhere a handbell was ringing. Wally saw me down, offering no comment. The place was teeming with patients and visitors in heavy overcoats, crowding at the entrance. At the foot of the stairs I took my leave, saying I would be over soon again. He handed me a slip of paper. 'Get me this' he said. At the door I looked back. He was going back to his room, gripping the bannisters, head down.

Outside, everything looked wet under a watery sun. The rain had blown over. I saw a bathtub piled with laundry. Two fellows in brown boiler suits and Wellington boots stood resting, inmates or staff. They gaped after me, perhaps envious, for was I not passing out through the institution gates.

In a bar in Ballina I examined Wally's slip of paper. He wanted Stendhal's 'Le Rouge et le Noir' in English. His small precise hand had not changed since boarding-school days.

CHAPTER XXI

The Suicided Corpse

'Not looking well' . . . 'Not looking *too well* these days' . . . 'Not looking at all well yesterday' . . . 'Looking bad a fortnight ago' . . . 'Looking really bad a month back' . . . 'Looking *terrible* the other day' . . . 'Not looking himself (herself) *at all* recently' . . . 'NEVER LOOKING WORSE' . . .

This miserable antiphony of doom-laden prognosis and foreboding rang constantly in my ears and coloured even the alternative view, always less insistently presented, as a short uncertain summer before the long killing winter.

In great form . . . Looking in the best of health . . . Never looking better; these were merely relapses from the norm of ill-health and not to be trusted. The people weak as flies in winter, crawling about, burdened with life. Nerves and nervous-breakdowns seemed maladies peculiarly Irish.

Both my mother and Wally had nervous breakdowns.

Wally, volunatarily committed to a mental institution in Ballina, was to spend some time under observation and work on the institute farm; my mother wept for a whole day after agreeing that he should go. On the day of his departure for Hazlewood House, in the early afternoon, she took to her bed fully clothed. She patted the place beside her on the blue-and white counterpane with its farmyard design of scratching hens and crowing roosters, indicating that I should console. She wept quietly and miserably, as if she intended to weep a long time, her hair loose, hairpins falling out. The sun travelled slowly across the wallpaper, off the counterpane, and I held her roasting hand, wishing I were elsewhere. Nothing would ever change for the better. Would they be hard on him, rough on her boy, was he in good hands, would they understand his troubles, his needs, his silence? They would not. He would have to endure heavy manual work, unfamiliar faces, rough fare at table, there would be electro-shock treatment. My father had driven him there.

Out of Hazelwood House and even more taciturn than before, Wally left for an officer's cadet course in England. He would not march with the infantry or travel in a tank, be sick in a destroyer or worse still down in a submarine, no. It was up in the air, at night, for him.

My mother stayed in bed for two years. Then she became obese, inventing a nervous disease that would keep her with Wally: claustrophobia. She could not attend Mass any more. Crowded places did not suit her any more. No place that she had ever visited or been happy in, could be visited again; her friends were reduced to a select few, in time they would become even fewer. She knew no friends. The house was a 'disgrace'; she felt 'ashamed' of it, house-work was 'beyond' her. Her manner became distant, eccentric. Now she spent long hours staring out the window at the clouds. A priest came once a year to give her Holy Communion. Dr Sheehan called with a heavy black labrador. The animal came wheezing into the bedroom, collapsed on the rug, shaking the floor. Dr Sheehan sat on the edge of the bed and said 'Now Dilly . . .'

He could find nothing wrong with her and retired baffled. The war raged on in Europe to the tune of Melachrino's strings, the bounce of the Glen Miller orchestra, the signature-tune for In Town Tonight, Forces Favourites, the rumbas of Edmundo Ross. My mother stayed in bed.

My father tolerated it. This was her way, he would not gainsay it. She was happy in her own way, he said. From her sick-bed she dominated him and the house. Her voice became fainter and fainter. My father had an off-hand way with bills; he would impale them on a wire skewer and forgot them. Creditors called. For six months my father dreamed of winners, broke the local bookie, who called and asked for more time to pay. The war, which would come to an end before Wally could go into action, with the night-fighters, raged on.

When Wally came home on leave in his officer's uniform, cap on the side of his head, my mother left her bed to be photographed with him in the garden, his limp hand resting on her shoulder as she sat on the edge of a wheelbarrow in a fur-coat and demi-veil. When Wally's leave expired, she went back to bed again.

There was nothing organically wrong with her, Dr Sheenan said; her nerves had gone against her. To be well again she must get out of bed, get on her own feet again, find outside interests.

She continued her life in bed. Existence without Wally wasn't any life at all. She would prefer to be dead, didn't want to live. Her voice became fainter, high-pitched; she was becoming him.

One day in spring towards the end of the war, my father, urged on not by one doctor but by two (a nerve specialist from Dublin), persuaded my mother to get out of bed, and booked a table for dinner at a nice hotel by the sea.

'Alright,' my mother said, resigned now, 'alright . . .' None of her clothes fitted her, a suitable ensemble had to be let out, a day was wasted ('she's perking up,' my father said, glad to see any sign of change). 'She'll be herself again,' old Mrs Henry said, 'Yewell suy.'

She left her bed, seemingly excited about the outing. A hired car called. She was weak on her feet, could hardly walk, but managed it outside, marvelling at the colours of the spring. But when she saw the sea she refused to go on. My father coaxed her, but she would not listen to reason; on she would not go, no argument could shift her. My father had to tell the taximan to turn round. My mother went back to bed.

A week later she could confess to me: 'Dan, I just couldn't go on. Something stopped me. It was the sea that separated me from Wally.'

That numbed slow time with my mother in bed, not even reading, her spirits sunk, her voice gone, sleeping much of the day, always sleeping, a resentful unconscious deep-breathing inert mound.

What did she want? Wings tipping over the sea, the sun in splendour on the water, all grief forgotten, Wally in his nightfighter performing a Victory Roll?

Bed as reassurance, it did not seem to rest her: 'I'm dead tired,' she said often. 'I'm tired out, *exhausted*, Dan.'

In that sluggish time, when my mother had ample time to sleep, she had a nightmare of Jus dead. He had been the go-between when she and my father were courting, and had himself married the next youngest of my mother's six sisters. In the dream a naked male corpse sweated on a table in a windowless room. Two months later, Jus gassed himself and had to be identified in the morgue by his eldest son. The body was sweating, the windowless room was the Dublin morgue. My mother's dream was out, the sweating corpse was Jus, her sister's suicided Flemish husband.

She celebrated the end of the war in her own way, by getting out of bed. Wally was in Scotland now studying to be a land surveyor. Nullamore was sold. My parents moved to Dalkey, outside Dublin. I entered into employment with Delaney in Irish Assurance. I found a flat in a wing of Howth Castle. Lord Talbot de Malahide became my land-lord. I was permitted to take rotted timber from the estate. Exley came from Anglesea Street on his bicycle and bored me with his long silences. There was a cromlech in the grounds. Walking below the rhododendron cliff was like walking in the high Himalayas. I left at 8.00 a.m. every morning for Delaney's office in Upper O'Connell Street, going by train to Amiens Street, a dark echoing place. The years rolled on. Time went by.

CHAPTER XXII

The Thirteenth Man

In the dead part of that year, one of those pallid onyx-and-opal days that descend so frequently on the grey capital, I was making my way with no particular purpose in mind towards the Rotunda. Approaching from the opposite direction I saw the last person I'd have expected to find walking abroad. In a suit of light blue Irish tweed with matching waistcoat, a dark blue shirt and matching bow tie, not exactly sauntering but drifting with purpose in tan brogues in a southerly direction came Senator W. B. Yeats in person.

He was noticed but unrecognized, the pedestrians made way for him; country people up for the day, shopping in Clery's; children, sucking ice-cream cones ignored the shock of white hair, the imposing presence, the absented manner. His demeanour was that of a man accustomed to having his own way. The texture of his lips, pressed tightly together, might have belonged to another face. And where was he bound for?

Too late for lunch at the Arts Club. When he entertained Olivia Shakespear upstairs, after the Voronoff operation, the building shook, malicious tongues reported. It was the wrong day for a matinee at the Abbey. Fitzwilliam Street was far away, and I could not see the Senator taking public transport. Was he just taking the air?

The air!

With tidal filth shifting about on brackish waters, on the ebb, the river stank of coal-slack and diarrhoea, cabbage and oil-slick all the way to Clancy Barracks. It wasn't the Garavogue.

At times now he would be at home in Riversdale in Rathfarnham, or away at Menton, the Athenaeum in

138

London or the Chantry House, banqueting at the Irish Academy, making impromptu speeches. He moved about.

I followed him now as if carried along in this great man's wake.

He passed the fruit-sellers and flower-sellers at Nelson's Pillar, not turning aside as expected at North Earl Street when we came to the junction of O'Connell and Abbey Street, where a man on a box was roaring. The city people recognized him, for they went by, bending their heads and smiling. Yeats created a stir. I followed on rubber soles, fifteen paces to the rear. He did not resemble Jack, his younger brother, known to me by sight. He came to a halt outside the Grand Central Cinema and began studying the stills through quizzing-glasses, as strange a sight to see as a giraffe with its head in the tree-tops. Then he stepped up to the ticket office and, bending, spoke to someone within.

Opposite, at the Astor, 'Der alte und der junge König' was running, with Emil Jannings and Werner Hinze. The conflict between Prussian Frederick and his son. The Grand Central was offering 'The Thirteenth Man', a tale of the occult. Perhaps the Senator was going to the wrong cinema?

The broad tweed-clad back straightened up. He pocketed his change, examined his ticket, passed resolutely in. I advanced to the grille. An elderly woman sat within.

'The same as my father,' I said.

She issued a balcony ticket, which I paid for, depriving myself of lunch (Bovril and Gold Grain biscuits at Robert's Café in Suffolk Street), gladly, and followed Yeats in.

He was slowly ascending the carpeted stairs. The empty photographic eyes of the Hollywood stars watched him grandly doing so. Robert Taylor and Spencer Tracey, Ida Lupino and Sonja Henie. Our feet made no sound on the thick carpet.

A female hand, white with a purple ring, held aside the heavy brown drapes, beckoning. The poet, sensing someone following, turned and looked directly at me. An elderly usherette held open the curtain. Behind the strong protective spectacles two small dark eyes were turned inward like those of a lizard, the expression in them veiled and secretive. He saw me, yet he did not see me, his mind on other things.

The pale hand disappeared, the drapes fell; on the other side the broad accent complained that he could not see. I waited a moment, surprised by the accent, then followed.

The auditorium lay in darkness.

Then a torch-beam moved along the rows of empty seats. I heard the voice droning. He could not see, he was thankful for the light. The elderly usherette conducted him to the front row of the balcony. A young one flashed her torch on my ticket. 'You are with him?'

'No.'

'Follow me.'

'Gladly.'

I followed her, half-turned towards me, directing the beam at my feet. I chose a seat immediately behind Yeats, two rows back.

The cinema was empty. At once the gauzy veils began to part and the false aurora borealis appeared, shimmering on a black and white caption, the screen flickering with many grainy dots and scratches. Yeats sighed and cleaned his spectacles, as smiling Dutchwomen in clogs and scolloped bonnets posed in a tulip field, the great sails of windmills turned slowly, clouds were reflected in canals, a tram in Delft crossed a hump-backed bridge, the sea beat against the dykes, and again plain Dutch faces were wreathed in smiles. It went on. I paid little attention.

Then a rooster crowed silently and flapped its wings and music started as first Nationalists and then Republicans in forrage caps were brandishing rifles and running up a hill in Catholic Spain, giving the clenched fist salute. Then the Cross was slowly falling from a church dome and a long line of refugees with their possessions and children were walking their way along an endless road. Guns and fists were pointed to the clear sky and in Madrid General Franco addressed a crowd from a balcony draped in flags. Against all this carnage the noble head of Yeats was outlined, and whenever the turbulence of the sound-track allowed, I heard him groan and sigh, shifting his long legs in evident discomfort.

Then that too ended and the trailer for a knockabout comedy began, with a noisy couple breaking dishes against a wall and shouting abuse at each other. But before long the cloaked lady held aloft the torch of liberty, spluttering with false flames for Columbia Films, and a document was shown, signed by the censor (Montgomery), passing the feature as fit for public showing.

The tall figure before me gave no sign of boredom, shifting about, crossing his legs and sighing as before. What I had suspected seemed to have been confirmed. He had come to the wrong cinema and was looking at the wrong film, which was, it so happened, dull beyond belief. But he stayed on. Absurd figures postured, rolled their eyes, a fog hid them up to the waist, the full moon disappeared behind clouds.

Three-quarter way through, when beyond hope of ever recovering, it did begin to improve, marginally. But Yeats had seen enough. With one final sigh he rose to his feet, and the older usherette came flying with her light to direct him out. His seat banged back. I smelt tobacco from him. 'I cannot see,' Yeats said. Then the usherette led him out.

I sat on until at last the film ended. The lights came on. Some patrons, evidently drunk, were sitting in various stages of disorder below. The light dimmed out, the programme began anew, aurora borealis, credits, Dutchwomen, dykes, a rooster crowing. I did not look at it, to hear it was bad enough. Finally I left. The two usherettes were taking the air, such as it was, on the landing. The older one had frizzled orange hair to match an extraordinary orange complexion and a vivid slash of lipstick. The younger was a peroxide blonde. Both were togged out in blue paramilitary-style uniforms with belts, brass buttons down the fronts, epaulettes and white gloves. Women in trousers looked odd. Both had large rumps. The younger one simpered at me.

I went out into pale damaged daylight, twilight already falling. A press of people blocked the entrance to the GPO. I walked fast towards the river, past bloated bronze statues of heroic females punctured with bullet-holes in the nipples. Seagulls flew over the bridge uttering a single cry. *Woe! Woe!* The tide was fully out. The stench was even worse than before. Sulphuric acid. The country people were hurrying for the long-distance buses on Arran Quay. Their children were already feeling queasy. Billboards flapped, a legless man played a mouth-organ. 'The Isle of Capri.' I could play it myself. I read the scrawled headlines:

APOSTOLIC BEN
PI XI URGES
BEN MUSS . . .

I felt sick. Yeats had long ago disappeared into the crowd. The Bovril sign bled all over College Green.

CHAPTER XXIII

The Girl on the Steps

Out walking one morning and encountering many orientals, elegant Chinamen carrying pressed pants and dark suits in plastic bags from the Lyk-Nu dry-cleaners, I made my way via Ranelagh and Charleston Road (tapping of a typewriter in a garden flat) into Belgrave Square.

At the triangle, old men of destitute appearance were creeping into the public urinal to their morning stools of repentance. A severed claw lay on the pavement, outside a dirty poulterer's shop. Dogs had fouled up Keegan's wall. The glazed eye of an eight-pound coarse fish stared from the cold slab. Rows of dead poultry and game hung head-down—a sad array of fur and feather. Amid the chill stench of entrails, a balding man wearing a long-suffering face, with a soiled and blood-stained white apron and Wellington boots, was forcing shut the heavy door of the cold-storage plant. It was spring.

A warm land-breeze blew the length of Palmerston Road, stirring the leaves of the chestnut trees. Once, after dark, I had seen a hedgehog on her hind legs in the long grass by the wall, heard her nibbling. Snouted like a little bull, with epileptic eyes. And once on a long summer evening a corncrake creaking rustily away behind the thin-spired church recalled my youth in Sligo. The square was used as a sportsfield by lumpy Protestant schoolgirls. Tied ankle to ankle, they ran screeching, falling on the slope with a startling display of functional underwear. In winter they played hockey, the plain ones chasing the ball while a pretty one sulked in goal.

Beyond Leinster Cricket Ground, on Rathmines Road, loomed the corroded dome of Our Lady of Perpetual Succour, over the roofs of Mount Pleasant Square. The east side, by the brown-stone Baptist Church, had always pleased my eye, the clouds piling above the low skyline of Castlewood Avenue. At a cross-roads by the traffic-lights, two bus-routes converged, 12's and 18's crossing at the junction. Mrs Fury and Mrs Maloney (who suffered from arthritis) let cold damp rooms overlooking the square. The 12's came from Cabra beyond the Rotunda over the river, from Oxmanstown Road near the Cattle Market and out between Mountjoy Prison and Grangegorman Mental Hospital, coming from the provisional terminus by Harold's Cross greyhound stadium and Mount Jerome Protestant cemetery.

18's travelled by Kenilworth Square into Rathmines, crossing over into Castlewood Avenue, rattling the Assistant State Solicitor's windows; and then by the traffic lights into Ranelagh—where the destitute old men had left the public lavatory and were now immersed in newspapers cast away on the public bench by the taxi rank (phone 22-22-22)—and so on via Chelmsford Road and Appian Way, Waterloo Road and the Institute for the Blind at Ballsbridge, into wide Pembroke Street and on out by the Royal Dublin Society sweepstake offices and grounds, leading to the provisional terminus in or near Simmonscourt Road.

The 12 busses came via O'Connell Street over O'Connell Bridge, by Trinity College railings into Dame Street, by Georges Street and Aungier Street into Camden Street, and so over the canal at Richmond Street and by Mount Pleasant Square and the Turkish Baths outside Ranelagh (shrouds for sale at the monastery gates under the railway bridge), out past Cowper Road to the provisional terminus under the horse chestnuts of Palmerston Park.

A Number 18, three-quarters empty, was crossing from the north side of the square, passing into Charleston Road by the old tramlines and by the two white lions couchant in reinforced cement outside Mrs Fury's house. The door of the end house corresponding to Mrs Fury's was newly painted in cyclamen red. Up the steps to this door went a pair of stylish long legs.

A 12, bound for Palmerston Park, slowed by the Baptist Church and halted opposite. A bold-faced strumpet in a leopardskin toque stared out familiarly. I stared back. She didn't know me from Adam. Up in his cabin the driver waited for the lights to change, allowing his eye to stray to the fair-haired one on the steps, the teddybear coat, the face averted. A gloved hand pressed the bell. Behind her the grey city was now all adrift in rain. Aware of eyes watching, she fumbled in her handbag, bit a pouting lower lip.

A muslin half-curtain was drawn aside a few inches and from above the newly painted door a coal-black face looked out. The strumpet in the leopardskin toque looked away. The traffic lights changed from red to orange, the driver released his air brakes, and began dragging with both hands at the steering wheel.

A pale palm was raised in greeting, wristwatch consulted, wide lips blew delicately on the blurred glass, uttering a word, a name (Jeanne?). White teeth were bared at the visitor in the rain.

Oh the lure of fur-clad young women, particularly in the morning! Particularly in the rain! A young woman wearing fur is a big cat, a very strong electric charge. An electric eroticism was in the air. Veils of rain drifted out of the sky.

The Number 12, its gears grinding ferociously, drew away with indicator still out, passing the cement lions on its way to the dripping chestnuts in Palmerston Park.

The cyclamen door glistened like lipstick. The half-curtains were white as the cuffs of the coloured man. Moisture glistened on the black spears of the railing. At one point a gap had been burst by a grey Volkswagen; a long line of tracks went over the grass to where it stood with its doors ajar, driven there at speed by some nightime drunkard. The tramlines were not yet dug up, though the tram company was long defunct. Awkward for cyclists.

I saw the blur on the glass over the red door. He was coming downstairs. Was it a 'maison de rendez-vous?' The visitor under her fur coat was nude as Vivienne Romance. It was pouring in Kimmage and Terenure, a deluge falling on Mount Argus. No one was about; it would rain all morning; they would be locked in each other's arms.

Rain continued to fall on the lush grass of the square, it glistened on the roof of the stalled Volkswagen, on the lions, on the black spears of the railing. As I went by in my soiled half-length military raincoat, the girl on the steps turned, looked out indifferently over the square, the bus receding. Her expression was thoughtful. She was going to a black man's bed at the wrong end of town.

The door opened and I caught sight of a well-built coloured man standing there in his white shirt, dark tie and trousers, polished black shoes. The visitor glided in and the door closed. Was there the slightest suggestion of a movement towards an embrace, just checked, before the door closed behind them? Were they embracing in the hall? The wet fur coat would bring with it some of the coolness and freshness of the morning, the visitor's lips would be cold, but not for long. She was very pretty. Still in the retina of my eye, an impression of young legs under a fur coat. Was the landlady ill and bedridden, away visiting relatives in the country, out shopping or dead? The closed door proclaimed: *None of your damned business.* No more movement of the half-curtain, no outcry from the hall, no outraged landlady in slippers and curlers showing the beautiful visitor out. Was she chewing her lower lip, being helped out of her fur, giving grinds to a man from Mauritius, Jamaica or Port of Spain, studying at Surgeons, or to a coloured Trinity student from Natal? Or the other way round, he helping her? She had brought no text books. Was it a reciprocal arrangement, she helping him and he helping her? Or a love assignation? The hour (10 a.m.) left both possibilities open. Belgrave Square was deserted, the rest of the city at work. Weighed in the balance, hours for study, time for love, the beauty of the visitor would turn the scales away from books and towards bed; her pose, composure, fumbling in handbag, pouting of lower lip, the hour of the day, her allure, her clothes, even the discomfort of the rain, all implied shelter, the warmth and closeness of bed. Sexual emancipation implied readiness.

I passed the sedate homestead of the Assistant State Solicitor, a legal man of innocuous address. In cords, double-vented tweed jacket and tan brogues, I had heard him make a largely inaudible address to Justice O'Hagen at the murder trial of the South African Mohangi. I entered Rathmines Road, thinking of a glass of Macon at Searson's on Portobello Bridge. A single-decker was turning off for Ballyboden. The monster columns swooned against the strangely elevated facade of Our Lady of Perpetual Succour. Behind celery stalks in a greengrocer's window was a box of avocado pears. Strange fruit, for Rathmines. Nutritive growth.

Black babies were being pushed around in prams by young Irish mothers. The rain had blown over and a weak sun shone. I thought of the Arab Emirs filling their harems, not with Berber girls but, in bi-annual raids of rape and rapine girls from the households of Christian Spain.

The young women pushing prams had kind faces. Take the baby out of the pram and let the lady see the fish. I noticed a white mouse in a cage. Now back there beyond the implacable church, the thick lips that had blown on glass were clamped on hers; a bolt shot home, eager black hands found willing whiteness.

Venue, fie! Most gross domination as ever I heard. O, the staccato, while you live, sir, note that.

CHAPTER XXIV

The English Major

You, nameless as yet, walked into St. Stephen's Green under the columns of the Grafton Street gate. HARTSHILL on one side, LADYSMITH on the other, TALANA COLLENTO, what did it mean? And now you were walking in dim retreating afternoon light under a thundery sky threatening rain. You cross the little humpback bridge. I walked behind you, I didn't know you. You wore something close-fitting in grey, your head uncovered (the long stylish legs in nylon had a perceptible tide-line of dark hair), you crossed into Leeson Street. A nun was walking on the roof of Vincent's Hospital, a lone Sister of Charity going to and fro, to and fro, the patient coif moving sedately among the chimney-stacks; she sailed so securely, so high up, I could only pity her. From there she could see the mountains, if she cared to look, lift up her eyes, even see the Hellfire Club. I went past the Holy House or Chapel-of-Rest on Lower Fitzwilliam Street. Behind me, where the street ended, the mountains began. I looked in. The chapel was empty. I walked in the direction of Ballsbridge, heading for the Royal Dublin Society to collect a book on Daumier. They were holding it for me. I saw a sign painted on a wall: DOWN WITH THE IRISH RULING CLASS, LACKEYS &GOMBEENS OF ENGLISH IMPERIALISM.

In the library I saw Ussher sitting at a table with piled up books. I did not disturb him. The street outside was like a country road in winter littered with clay and horse-dung from the regular passage of show-horses entering and leaving the show-grounds. As a child I had been sick there, full of ice cream and fudge, my barbered head like an iron cap. I waited at the bus-stop. A young blonde woman in a close-fitting grey rollneck pullover, ochre leather skirt and brown boots, waited before me. Presently a Dalkey bus came. The blonde girl went upstairs. I followed her. A country fellow made room for her, saying 'Sorry.' She sat, causing a sensation among the young countrymen up for the Horse Show. Her breasts were visible through the thin material, she had long hair, a pretty face. Young riders went by below, their mounts uneasy in the traffic. A lorry drew abreast, tightly packed with beasts bound for the abbatoir. The bus crossed the bridge; bursts of unseemly mirth from the three countrymen were answered by explosions of mirth from the two in the back. The fellow who sat beside the cause of it all was bottling it in, going purple in the face. I watched an elderly man leaving the bar below, followed by a young fellow, both bearing pints. The young lad's face was pale, he held onto the spikes of the railing. It was like in the country. Horse-dung on the roadway, morning intemperance. The blonde girl, embarrassed by the nudging and tittering, left at Waterloo Road, descending to the platform looking as embarrassed as if surprised in bra and panties. The country fellows craned their necks to see her go.

'Begod sheda' kum in first!'

'Paddy wanna'd giddyup on'er!'

The man with the high-coloured face: 'Oh begob the hard Paddy!'

'You'd be right if you said ye came up for the Show.'

The countrymen, leaning forward now, becoming serious, were talking football, the All Ireland Final. By Trinity College railings I left the bus.

That same evening, walking to the Huguenot cemetery in Merrion Row, I saw you again. The long stylish nylon-clad legs went before me; even then we didn't know, even then you were walking away from me, and even then I was following.

You had an escort; not exactly linking arms but walking close together with shoulders touching, a tall well-matched couple over for the Horse Show, I thought. He wore check tweeds, a suit with double vents, and tan boots, a deer-stalker. You were all in grey, your hair uncovered as before. I followed by Bells' dry-cleaners, watched you enter the Shelbourne Hotel. Without thinking, I followed.

Standing by the reception-desk, the middle-aged well-set-up military man with a saltpetered outdoor complexion and frantic blue eyes was inquiring whether there was any post for Major McNair. As the receptionist turned to look, I went past into the bar. You followed with Major McNair. A voice used to having its own way asked for a double Scotch and you asked for gin and tonic in an accent I could not place. I watched you.

You were not long in the bar. The Major spoke of changing for dinner, thinking of getting you undressed in a bedroom above. You went up in the lift, leaving your handbag behind. I was in the act of handing it over to the barman when you came back, alone. You were tall, a clown's face and hazel eyes. 'I think,' I began, as the bar began to rise up, full of tobacco smoke, whiskey fumes, expensive womens' scents, high hopes, into the dizzy evening air. You who would always be losing things, leaving a trail of lost objects behind, thanked me for that small service.

The Major waited in a bedroom upstairs, moving into the bathroom to bare his gums at the mirror, stroke his sandy moustache. He had frantic light-blue eyes; a frozen stare. He had come over to study Irish horse-flesh. It was apparent to me then that you might be prepared to ditch him. You could think of better things to do.

CHAPTER XXV

The Ghost of Emmett Grieve and the missing Ketch Joyita

My mother's bedroom: a large wide carpetless bare room with one uncomfortable high-smelling leather armchair, the last of a set purchased at discount from Jack Ellis, in a corner, near the mound of old newspapers, mostly *Irish Times*, and my mother sitting up in bed in a woollen cardigan with all the stitching gone in one arm, with that pointed stare and a smile directed at Olivia who was hearing for the first time mother's high sing-song.

'Is this Olivia?'

My father had been mowing in the garden, knowing we were coming. Both of them had aged. The two-storey house seemed empty now. They occupied the upper floor while a family who never appeared occupied the basement. A flight of steps went up to the hall-door, then more stairs to their living-quarters. Too much for my overweight mother.

In the bedroom, three long windows overlooked the bay. The wind boomed all around the house, yachts were tacking towards Howth, the line of the harbour wall stretched to the north-east. From where I stood it would be possible to see the mail boats arriving and departing. I opened one of the windows and the sea with its smells came closer. My father brought in a tray with tea and Gateaux. They fussed over it. Was it strong enough? There was no cream. Would milk do?

'Of course,' Olivia said.

'Is it alright?' my mother asked.

'Perfect,' Olivia said. She was dressed in tartan slacks, a pullover and black beret, high-heeled boots. My father had never seen a young woman in trousers before, only horsey ladies with big backsides in riding habits.

'Grieve,' my father said, seated on an upturned orange

crate with his legs crossed. 'Now that's a funny kind of name—is it Welsh, or where does it come from?' Knowing full well where it came from, for I had told him so in letters.

'Sugar?' my mother offered.

'New Zealand,' I said from the depths of the stinking armchair.

'New Zealand!' my father repeated in mock-amazement, as if I'd said The Moon.

'That might mean anything,' my mother said, smiling at her new daughter-in-law, who, long stylish legs crossed and beret removed, was eating Gateau out of a saucer. 'She might be Scots for all we know.'

'She might . . .' my father said, doubtful about it.

'I am,' Olivia said, 'sort of. Both my parents are Scots.'

'There, you see,' my mother said.

'A wee bonny lassie!' my father cried.

'More tea, dear?' my mother asked, giving my father one of her looks. He was staring at Olivia and laughing. His 'wee' daughter-in-law stood 5–9 and weighed 138 pounds in the buff.

'What religion is she, may one ask?' my mother asked when Olivia was out of the room. My father was showing her the view from the attic.

'You may,' I said. 'She hasn't any that I know of. The parents are Presbyterians.'

'Presbyterians!' my mother said faintly.

'Scots Presbyterians,' I amended it, 'the worst kind.'

My mother looked out of the window and sighed. Silence.

'It doesn't matter,' my mother said. 'She's a nice girl. Well brought up. One can see that. You might have been landed with a flippertygibbet.'

'I might.'

My father and Olivia came laughing back into the room. They had made up two beds for us. We drew them together, opened the window wide. Airs from the garden, the sky, flowers in a bowl. There was no other furniture in the room. It was a perfect bedroom.

'Oh, this air, it's not true,' Olivia said, sitting up naked in bed. 'It's Raglan, only stronger.'

Odour of seaweed and brine all night long, odour of new-mown grass, cut flowers, odour of space; all night the house swam through space as dogs barked in the quarry. The Dalkey night with her was strange, yet we were home.

Next morning before I had opened my eyes, recognising the sound of my father's stop-and-start method of mowing without a catcher, conserving his strength, we heard Sunday church bells ringing everywhere. Breakfast was ready. My mother brought in tea. When Olivia appeared dressed at the window my father called up to her. She had given him a present of a gold tie-pin, with a turquoise inset. Already he was addressing her as 'Livvy'. A sweet image of a girlie, a wee bonny lassie! My father, an impressionable man where good-looking girls were concerned, was already struck with her. Had he expected me to bring back some slack-mouthed whore?

We drank Guinness in a run-down bar. Out in the bay in a hired rowing-boat I watched the church spires of Dun Laoghaire diminish and the hills beyond the town put on more bulk; ranges of white clouds drifted over County Wicklow. I dropped lures over the side for mackerel.

'I like them,' Olivia said.

'They like you too,' I said, raising and lowering the lures. The current dragged, it was difficult to feel a catch.

'I had a dream last night,' she said. 'A dream that Emmett came back.'

She told me the dream. It was at Auckland airport. He was flying in on such a lovely day. They were waiting, the Grieves. Olivia saw the glimmer high up, like a silver fish in the blue sky. They watched it come in as though it were an ordinary flight arriving. She didn't know what to expect when it touched the runway, burst into flames and a winged horror come breaking out, a black Emmett appear. It circled, came in, touched down, taxied in, quite normally. The steps were pushed up, the door opened and the passengers began disembarking.

'I recognised him by the way he walked,' Olivia said. 'He wore a tall hat but carried no luggage, no brief-case even, nothing. Waving, if you please, an outsize Stetson. It was Emmett alright, my long-lost brother whom we hadn't seen in fifteen years. He was all grainy and colourless like a photo that's faded, walking with the others in a kind of mist. It was most odd and disturbing on this strangely bright unreal day to see my dead brother come towards us, not hurrying, carrying his hat. We were waiting at the barrier. My mother had begun weeping.

'He came right up to us. I was so happy to see him, grinning and holding this outsize Stetson. My mother was becoming smaller and smaller, weeping, her eyes shining. Emmett spoke all our names: Mom and Pop, Glen and Sis. I was still Sis. Did we embrace, shake hands? I forget. Mom just kept on weeping. Pop was growing younger and younger the more he looked at Emmett who was saying very little, just grinning from ear to ear as if this was the best joke in the world. He'd brought no baggage because he wasn't staying, apparently. In photos his nose turned up, but it didn't really. He was very calm. And then I was crying because he was back. We asked where he had been all those years. He clapped the Stetson onto his head, tilting it over one eye, looked at me and winked, those bright amused eyes watching. "Oh, I've been around," he said. He was a real grinning villain.'

Olivia had the collar of her seersucker up. It was cold in the bay. A beam of sunlight lit Howth Head. Below us, green water, stuff streaming down.

'I was only twelve then,' Olivia said. 'I mean when he drowned, disappeared, went missing. In the dream he would have been thirty-one . . . supposing the dead become older. Or do they always remain the same? Supposing he was dead. I'd loved him very much. And he me, I suppose, being the youngest and all that. Mom loved no one else but him, as she made quite clear. Certainly she didn't love me.'

I tried to recall where New Zealand was situated, as I rowed to new fishing grounds off the Forty Foot. To one side, alone among the rocks, a grossly fat nude man, who seemed to possess female sex organs, lowered himself slowly down into the water.

Near the Outer Circle, almost off the globe, were two chop-shaped islands, the southern oceans all around. One family, more tightly together than most countries, a small country divided in two in the southern seas. Ben Boucher's long-lost brother Denny had worked there as a doctor, going between the islands—until his ketch was discovered crewless 800 miles off course, the fire gone out in the engine room and an awning rigged up aft, as if one had survived. What had happened to the Doctor and his native crew? Sacked by privateers, run aground on one of the atolls, or the ketch looted and them abandoned there, or simply eaten by cannibals? Nothing was too strange. The Doctor had a gammy leg, wounded at Anzio beach. And the name of the ketch, as I rowed, pulled, watched Olivia trawling, came back to me: The *Joyita*.

I pulled, facing Olivia, just a nose and hair now emerging from the seersucker. Water and air were cold, the tide on the turn. Such opaque peace.

CHAPTER XXVI

Billy Grieve

From my own imperfect memory, from no notes, from distractions and places, from my love of her, from her own re-tellings, emerges this rigmarole: her past that is more real than my own.

A large town house, all the windows closed, with one exception. A large gabled roof and encircling pillared verandah. The phantom Everett sisters pass in their old Buick. Dr Wallace drives drunk through the garage door. Olivia is studying her sick face in the full-length mirror of the dressing-table. A spider is crawling across the windowsill, incey-wincey, signifying rain; two enormous birds alight silently in the banana tree outside as her father, old man Grieve, dressed in white flannels and a narrow boater hat encircled with a thin blue ribbon, leaves for the bowling-green. The fig trees are shaking in the garden. Dr Wallace's wife does not understand him, he is Irish, their marriage has gone sour. Old Grieve disapproves of Dr Wallace. His daughter Georgina masturbates in the parked car with a girl friend, dreaming of Van Johnson pulling faces under a shower.

The figs are rotting under the fig trees in the garden, dislodged by the descent of enormous birds, the banana fronds fidgeting and scratching, at five a.m. her father runs hot water from the bathroom tap.

The sash is being drawn up in his daughter's room and the sun shines on the wooden floorboards. Motes of dust dance in the sun, and the old wizened Maori woman passes with a bundle on her head. Her mother rises every morning at six. Father already up and dressed, bringing tea with the Auckland morning paper. Her parents have separate rooms, not having slept together since Olivia's birth. Mrs Gwen

Grieve is not present in the room for long periods, but goes from room to room sighing, all her life since her daughter's birth sighing, her existence one long sigh. Or playing the piano by an open window. Or suddenly leaving, walking out of the house at night. On sweltering summer days they hear the pigs screaming down in the slaughterhouse. And in the untended garden, under the palm trees, droppings of enormous birds, or figs rotting on the grass, and you giggling with Stephanie Weir in the bamboos.

That place, your home, I can't imagine it. You lived there in a house I cannot quite see, walking in an overgrown garden in the heat. Banana trees fidget and scratch, mosquitoes sting, a small black-faced Maori woman watches you like a monkey. 'Miss Olliva!' A tree is uprooted in a hurricane and re-planted upside-down as a sign to German observation planes, Nazi secret agents up to their tricks in Auckland among the Jews.

As a child, sick, you lie in your mother's bed, a large cold bed, severe and white, a 'strict' bed, looking up at the large ornate wardrobe, the drawers own one side, where in the darkness of the hanging cupboard, your mother's scent clings, 'autocratic' like dark wood. Sometimes you crouched in there, the hems of the dresses touching the tips of your ears.

Her father gave her money to have her spurs removed. Her mother's scent mixes with the dark smell of the wood. The bed is also made of the same dark wood. 'I don't remember a time when I could climb onto it with ease,' you admitted. When her mother was in the room, wearing the scent she used, the sash window drawn up, she would play early music on the piano, while news of the war came over the wireless in the kitchen. Her strict mother dropped the definite article for the Maori servants in the kitchen. 'Run into kitchen Paulus and bring pail.' 'Run into hall Paulus and fetch Master's hat.' A wizened little Maori man, burnt like a cinder, lived in a hovel.

In the bedroom: the dressing table is practical and ugly, on either side of the full-length mirror are drawers, the bottom one being difficult to open, full of mementoes of bygone times: bundles of love letters tied with ribbons, craftwork done by Emmett in kindergarten, photographs of people dispersing from a group, Olivia's paintings and drawings. The love letters were from her undemonstrative husband, leaning at this moment towards the bias down at the bowling-green.

Olivia is painting her eyes, looking at herself in the mirror, wondering whether she is beautiful. She has a crush on a girl called Elizabeth Ann Runciman. On the highest branch of her favourite tree they carve their initials: EAR and OG in identical hand-writing. When Elizabeth Ann caught measles Olivia Grieve caught them too. In the deep end of the swimming-pool, underwater, with eyes open, they kiss, the light from above transforming Elizabeth Ann, long black hair swirling about her head, her features sweetly blurred and mouth puckered for the kiss.

When the wind was in the wrong direction there came wafting over the house the smell of uncured sheepskin from the warehouses, tannery stenches, stale dairy smells, milk gone off, dust in summer, the setting lotions at Woolf's hairdressers and the smell of sweet and sickly eggs on the turn. Hear the hiss of tongs, the smell of singed hair. And her cold mother, for whom it is always the one time, the time when all clocks stopped the day Emmett drowned, a season of mourning and tears, standing always at some window, anxious, attentive, waiting. Or playing at the piano, 'Sweet Bird of Love Divine'.

Jim Roach went beserk and brained his 'ravishingly beautiful' young wife with a bird-cage stand, leaving two orphans. Hedy Roach, neé Schermbrucker, who had liked to show around wedding photographs, a child-bride. Her father, ill with TB, was meanwhile coughing the last of his life away, a gaunt brown man convulsed under the sheets.

Dr Wallace played golf with his wife, went fishing alone at the rivermouth, saw a shark's fin, threw a stone at it. He went to the club alone, drove violently back at midnight, right smack into the garage, the car backfiring and him roaring, slamming on the brakes a metre from the end wall. And then the banging of the car door, and then silence. Hedy Roache, neé Schermbrucker, had a pale skin, dark eyes and hair and looked like Hedy Lemarr. Dr Wallace had removed her tonsils.

A strong alto female voice sang 'Compapa, compapa!' 'Olivia,' Miss Weir declared, 'has almost genius.' Staring at the sheet-music she plays de Falla's 'Ritual Fire Dance' and sang to her own accompaniment the Burial Song from Verdi's 'Aida'. A tall upright woman with a masculine face who would cross her legs decorously; she wore a felt hat pinned with a badge on the side, the Girl Guide Mistress. She played Incey-wincey-spider-climbing-up-the-spout, a woman of 'frightening morality in a blue uniform.'

Jim Roach was the son of wealthy parents, descendents of wool merchants, friends of the Everetts, both families being on visiting terms with the Grieves.

In those days, the mid-1940s, Jewish refugees came from Europe to settle in Auckland, obliged to leave homelands, trades and professions behind, some of them making new careers from former hobbies. Old Grieve admired those Jews who had found jobs and settled into the community, because they worked hard and were 'steady', a word of high praise from him. They were, he said, a stabilising influence on New Zealand society in general. Olivia had only a vague idea why the Hubschers and Hubermanns and Haydns had left Hungary and Rumania and Germany to come and settle in Auckland, of all places, since she herself was impatient to leave it as soon as possible. The Jewish refugees known to the Grieves were: Sam Liebermann, Professor of Greek and Latin, Otto and Susie Hubscher, the

husband a violinist, his wife a machinist in a factory, Irene
Laisarowicz, who became a photographer and called herself
'Miss Price', Mimi Deutsch who started a factory for
manufacturing bags and gloves, two Hungarians, George
Haydn and Irma Lucas, an Austrian, John Hubermann;
and two with Irish names who were hardly Irish, Frank
Kennedy (photographer) and Eddie Ring (clothing trade).

Olivia, born in Dunedin on the South Island, of Scots
Presbyterian parents who had emigrated around the turn of
the century, had lived most of her life in Auckland where
she was brought up, the youngest in a family of three, an
only daughter. Her parents had wanted another boy; they
called her Billy.

CHAPTER XXVII

Gussens and the Groper

Nick Gutheridge was in love with her. His hair was cut short 'like a convict's'. He sat at the wheel of the truck, transporting cooking utensils and furniture to the beach for the summer vacation. The setting sun, much enlarged, shone through the skin of his protruding ears, 'lighting up the blood vessels'. Tongue-tied, looking through the insect-smeared windscreen, changing gears, afraid to say her name, humming to cover his embarrassment, the engine fainting and stalling, bedding and kitchen provisions piled up on the back, with family retainers (Maori) mounted on the luggage, singing, the dust of the track filling all nostrils and throats, the overheated engine panting and stalling. At the beach, the tongue-tied and overheated Nick Gutheridge pitched the bell-tent a hundred yards from the sea. Shadows on the canvas at night. Barbecues on the beach, incey-wincey-spider climbing up the spout.

Sunset over vast landscapes and then the beginnings of hot nights, with trains shunting, squeal of metal getting into motion again, hiss of escaping steam, the sound of cattle bellowing on their last night on earth and the Baptist bell banging away into the small hours. She and Stephanie Weir, with skirts high, climbed the picket fence into forbidden ground, saw light shining in the ground-floor of the Stewarts' house and there was Syd the diving champion naked from the waist down, elbows moving, hidden hand at crotch, engaged in 'some secret male thing'. They crept away, mystified.

Dr Wallace's drunken car can be heard returning. The Everett sisters drive past in their phantom Buick, the leaves of all the trees are shaking, Miss Weir sings hoarsely the Burial Song from 'Aida' and Olivia's mother is playing the piano by the open window at Number 23 Konini Road. They play games of forfeits. The Murder of Paddy's Black Pig and 'Here-is-a-thing and a very pretty thing, whatshallwedowiththisveryprettything?' holding up garters, ties and shoes while tongue-tied suitors are ridden like horses around the room, ears flaming. The players are blindfolded and then just the touch of lips. Two personal articles are held up together, 'what shall we do with this very pretty thing?'

Averting her face and pushing to her seat at the concert in the City Hall, obliged to pass the false friend, the girl who has only called at Number 23 in order to see Emmett, trembling and hoping desperately for some sign of gentleness, she goes to her place. She is sixteen and going to Otago Girls' High School was 'a time of prolonged physical discomfort'. Obliged to wear an awful blue uniform that came back damp from the laundry. 'They always seemed to be damp. Piles of stuff with that awful laundry smell.' She has her first period late, crouched over the desk, pouting and shivering, rather remote now, like all other daughters who know their time has come. The human reproductive organism's precarious journey through life has begun, deadly red blossoms, dying goldfish hang head-down, their entrails becoming fungoid in cloudy water, in a bowl entrusted to her. Boys in the garden are blowing up frogs, figs are rotting under the fig trees; the leaves of all the palm trees shaking in the garden. The scent is of pine, roses, earth, the watered garden at sundown, pepper trees, bougainvillea, syringa, the tumid twilight and pigs screaming in the slaughterhouse down in the banana groves by the river. They covered their ears but, running away, could hear them screeching.

She played the doomed girl in Anouilh's 'Antigone' in an amateur production at the City Hall in aid of the Red Cross. The fellow she played opposite wore grey worsted tights and the press photograph showed a large stain at the crotch, stage-fright no doubt. He pressed the back of his hand to his brow in a gesture of classical anguish. Olivia in an ill-cut period costume sat tragically looking out through a papier-maché castle window.

A big game hunter appeared in Auckland looking not for six but a dozen beautiful girls to appear in a jungle film he said he intended to make. You showed me the press clipping.

WANTED—12 GIRLS, LOVELY, BUT BRAVE
(They Will Face Jungle Terrors)

'QUALITIES undreamed of by Hollywood,' ran the yellowed text, 'are demanded by Mr Clyde Gussens, big game hunter, in search of 12 New Zealand girls to take part in a forthcoming film of Central Africa.

'Mr Sussens told our reporter in Auckland that the girls must be: tough enough to face a charging elephant; calm in the face of unexpected crocodiles; poised in the presence of poisonous snakes; and willing to travel in malarious and sleeping-sickness areas. The girls must be good-looking, 100 per cent physically fit, well-educated and with good voices.

'We want no dolls or la-di-dahs. The girls must be able to take it.'

A photograph showed the head of a wild-eyed schemer with lips parted under a Don Ameche moustache, with close-set eyes and lobeless ears. He didn't look like a big game hunter; he was up to no good. Her parents advised Olivia not to apply. She applied, but nothing came of it. Gussens, or Sussens, left Auckland. Olivia continued to work in Bat Whitnell's office, dreaming of London and the stage. Six years before I met her, might she not have been despoiled by the wild-eyed Gussens in some equatorial jungle?

'Billy' Grieve walked along Queen Street and looked into the antique shops in Karanghape Road. She felt awkward and unloved, dropped things. In the Knox Church she no longer stood between her brothers Glen and Emmett for her younger brother Emmett (aged 18) had drowned in the

Tasman Sea when she was twelve. They heard the Rev. Herron thundering out his hellfire sermons. She rode a bicycle on Ninety Mile Beach and threw fruit at Pelerous Jack, the dolphin that followed the ship. At Russell in the far north the returning boats ran up a flag to show those waiting on the shore that swordfish had been killed. She swam at St. Kilda and St. Clair and in wild Pegasus Bay.

Her parents were not hitting it off. They no longer spoke to each other. The home atmosphere was chilly. Her mother was in constant touch with the dead. With hair crawling, Olivia heard the wind panting in the great organ of the Knox Church, saw a skeleton stir in deep water, knelt in an oaken pew with moon-faced Presbyterians. Spirit mediums were consulted. A glass serving dish broke itself neatly into four even parts, a chair turned itself a fraction, a dog came into the living room and barked at Emmett's image on the sideboard, ectoplasm curled from the wall.

She fished with boy-friends off Whangarei Reef, won swimming races; cups and silverware accumulated. Her father rarely smiled. Her mother never laughed. Her first boy-friend shaved his hairy legs. He hardly spoke, would swim for miles and she adored him. The bones of Emmett Grieve were rolling about at the bottom of the Tasman Sea which was wide and the deepest in the world.

Olivia changed her boy-friends as often as her religion. Gauche suitors invaded the house while her mother went from room to room sighing. The body was never recovered. Lost, presumed drowned, and officially dead after seven years.

'Billy' was obliged to swim in the public baths at Auckland. Storms blew in from the Pacific and from Tasman Bay and thousands of little needles stung her face and shoulders, scattering over the surface of the pool where she swam alone. Two lengths and home in the rain where a meagre supper was set out for her. She went hungry to bed, wondering if her mother loved her. If so, she restrained it.

Love, even the signs of affection were hard won.

One night when she was in her room preparing for bed, a groper came across the flat roof in tennis shoes, whispering her name by the window. She went naked to the air, wrapped herself in the curtain, asked who it was and what he wanted. 'Nothing,' a voice said. She knew him. A fellow who looked like Mungo Park. She herself was a tall naked girl who didn't know her own mind. 'Just stand there,' the voice said. A hand crept through the open window and into the curtain and touched her. She stood there, unable to see his face, hearing him breathing. After a while the hand was withdrawn and the voice said 'Now I can go to bed, Olivia Grieve.' She did not hear him going back across the roof. She put the light out and went to bed. 'I think he must have been as simple as myself,' Olivia said.

At 23 Konini Road, her mother went from dining room to lounge, from lounge to bedroom, arranging brushes and combs, sighing at open windows, for her heart wasn't in it, her heart was broken, had been broken long ago when Emmett drowned. Only bits and pieces remained. Suitcases remained packed, as if ready for a journey.

She heard the air panting in the great organ of the Knox Church, a glass serving-dish broke into four segments, a dog backed out of the living room as ectoplasm curled from the wall, and of Emmett Grieve, in Air Force uniform, squinting into the sun, mounted on the sideboard, one could not tell how he might have been at forty or fifty; at eighteen he looked *unformed*.

They had a weekend cottage at Raglan, called 'batch' or 'crib'. Born in Dunedin on the South Island, she lived most of her life in Auckland. When she was twelve her younger brother Emmett was drowned in the Tasman Sea. At sixteen she went to boarding school at Otago Girls' High.

She had three different names at home, 'Billy' to her

father, 'Shell' to her cold mother, 'Sis' to her dead brother; none of them were her own and 23 Konini Road did not feel like home. Glen married a Baptist, Elaine Tutt. A small crabby-faced man walked in the garden; it was her father-in-law. Glen had bought a revolver to scare off a rival. Old man Grieve, suited and cravatted, with the temperature into the high nineties, sat in a rocking-chair on the porch facing his surviving son; both of them invisible behind large newspapers, which they rustled at each other. A book came through the post for Olivia: *Ryder*, a waste of money her father thought. The rocking-chair tipped, the newspapers rustled, a partner—not dishonest, merely a fool—decamped with funds. Old man Grieve, obstinate as a mule, went it alone, all debts incurred would be repaid. Yet another burden was taken on and the spirits of Mrs Grieve, never very high, sank even lower. The dispirited woman sat at an open window, pressed down the keys, sang 'Bird of Love Divine,' or was it sweet bird?

'I don't understand you, Gwen.'

At vacation-time, when you returned, they came alive again for a time, only to settle back into apathy and settled gloom when you departed. Your life then was one constantly delayed departure.

Gwen Grieve sat by the open window, sang 'Once in a lifetime love's dream comes true' or alternatively 'I gave my heart to one man, loving as only woman can.' You walked back from the baths, ravenous. Your parents were nowhere to be seen. A meagre cold meal was set out. The house was empty. You read *Ryder*. Were you too clever for me?

You wept when you saw the Tasman Mountains because they were the last sight Emmett must have seen, choking out in the bay. You travelled by train to Te Araroa, the Bay of Plenty, after swimming trophies.

Gwen Grieve 'got bored' always arranging meals for old man Grieve alone, so particular in bib and tucker, prodding suspiciously at whatever was set before him, wanting to know what it cost.

'I don't understand you, Gwen.'

They moved to a hotel, dressed for dinner, outside the dining room old man Grieve ordered them to hold their stomachs in, toes slightly apart; drilled in this manner the Grieves sailed in. Meals were served by huge high-smelling half-castes. Gargantuan spreads impossible to get through, breakfast alone boasted nine courses. They ate sucking pig, Trevalli and Toheroa, Curried Crayfish, Paua Roe Patties, Baked Trevalli, greenbone deep-sea line fish, gropers, passion fruit, Chinese gooseberries, guavas, persimmons, oysters and pauas, mutton-birds, all good New Zealand things. The abundance made old man Grieve short of breath, bicarbonate of soda ended the meal. Maori waiters in scarlet uniforms served coffee in the lounge, occupied by commercial travellers. Impossible transients with scorched faces hung out of windows and waved to you, klaxons blared.

A sad-faced woman sat under a palm tree. A parrot-cage stood on a sundial. Organ music issued from the annex. One Saturday, Tom Taafe, the resident organist, fell dead of a heart-attack right in the middle of 'The Nearness of You'.

Gauche sun-scorched suitors invaded the hotel grounds. Presbyterians, Xian Scientists, Methodists, Baptists, never Roman Catholics, a religion representing less than ten per cent of the total population. A dark-complexioned sallow youth who looked like Mungo Park came from Greymouth; there was a doctor's son with shallow interests, loose dentures.

When Olivia came of age she sailed for London with her best friend Georgina Wallace. She was not to see her father again. Hand-held bunting, streamers made of pocket handkerchiefs tied together, would be the last she would see of him, growing smaller and smaller on the quayside, weeping as the liner moved out into the bay. She and Georgina Wallace were weeping their hearts out on the rails.

That was her past, part of it, as she told it to me, as I

remember it, or what I remember of it. For her twenty-fourth birthday I gave her a present of 'Wedding Preparations in the Country'. Born under Balance, she was Air, Libra, Venus in one of her hot storms. Libras can be tyrannical or conciliatory, blowing hot and cold, don't try to reason with them. She was generally as naked under the red dressing-gown as that courageous young lady of old Verona.

On her small turn-table she played Jacqueline Françoise, 'La Mer', Ravel, de Falla, Monteverdi. She wrote poetry. I believed her. I believed everything she told me. Was she too clever for me?

I had waited five weeks before phoning her. I could not forget her. I phoned the Yugoslav Embassy. A friend, I said, moving sideways like a crab, a good friend wanted to know some details of the French Cameroons. Silence on the other end. 'Fuck the French Cameroons,' you said. 'When are you coming over?'

'Isn't that what I'm telling you,' I said, 'I'm on my way.'

I was on my way. The pipes in the old 'Princess Maude', groaning deeply under the waterline, were manfully attempting to articulate your name. *OR-lave! Aucklove! Awk-awak! Or-leave! Oh-live!*

Go on.

CHAPTER XXVIII

The Poet Gabby Gall

Of her more recent past, the affairs of her more recent past, this emerged. She was making room for me, telling it to me as she knew it. Certain names recurred. Verna Naude, Anna Richter-Visser, Etricia Mocke, Eghard van der Hoven, Johannes Venter, Harry Ligöff—actors and actresses, I assumed, in Auckland, where I had never been.

She admired the actress who played Lysistrata. They met. Her name: Lydia Lindeque, a languid, sharp-faced woman with long black hair. Her husband was the novelist and poet Gabby Gall.

'A poet,' Olivia said. She had a special way of saying Poet. He was famous, at least in New Zealand, the Great Auckland Poet. He was overseas. Later Olivia wrote to him. He translated Lorca. She loved Lorca. She wrote Gabby Gall a fan letter, feeling admiration for him, almost adoration, wanting it to be love for the poet and novelist married to the languid Lydia Lindeque who played Lysistrata in the play by Aristophanes.

Gabby Gall answered her letter. He wanted her to fly to him. He was living in a fisherman's cottage near the beach at Tossa de Mar. He would pay half the air-fare.

She was in Paris. He sent her half the air-fare, rather less than half, the rest to be paid when she arrived.

She showed me his letters, digging them out of a trunk. He wrote in a large vainglorious scrawl. He wrote:
Calle Pablo Moreu 19, Tossa de Mar, Gerona.
10/4/53
My dear, You are a very naughty girl. You must not start overrating me sweet child . . .

The classical approach for long-range seduction; I did not bother to read it all. It was scrawled in hard pencil on notepaper headed Edinburgh International Festival, signed with his Christian name: Johannes.

But something had gone awry. A postal strike in France. She returned to London. He wrote again.
Same address. 1/9/53. My dear Olivia, We are indeed star-crossed. My heart gave quite a jump this morning when I saw the dear familiar handwriting. I am lonely here at Tossa de Mar and want to see you at all costs soon.

Again the offer to pay half the air-fare (total £28) to Barcelona. He was staying with a 'wonderful old couple' in a fisherman's hut on the beach for ten shillings a day all found, correcting early editions of his poetry for publication. He enclosed press clippings relating to himself, Dutch reviews. Parts that she should pay particular attention to were underlined in pink ink. Photographs of himself ('They Met in London'), with a moustache, receiving a cheque. 'You'll get beautifully brown—you'll dazzle my eyes more than ever. Surely your old Persian will let you have one day extra?' Olivia was his 'sweet child', his corporal (That's an order, corporal'). He described himself as 'a typical homme des lettres'.

She went to Tossa de Mar. It was a fiasco. She didn't like his hands. A monkey-man. She went to the beach with a younger man, leaving the poet working. A great hound appeared from nowhere, came bounding across the sand to dig a deep hole between them. It was a sign. They retired into an olive grove. She succeeded with him, where she had failed with the poet. After which she returned to London. Gabby Gall sent her a poem.

> Inhabit and bring
> To the pale shell your
> Body as an offering
> And a promise of life.

Waiting in an aching shell
For the hour of the delicate
And unashamed consumation.

Breaking with tender furry water
The pattern of dirt and brittle whiteness
To be caught in
Unleashed spirit of the pale cloud.

Dated 23 December 1953, Tossa de Mar.

Oh me, oh my, I see the little lady passing by. He wrote to her later, not often. She showed me the letters, since I'd asked to see them. 'If you want to,' she said, 'of course.' Postmarked from Tossa, Paris, Belgium, they were innocent enough. He was vain, wanted to impress her. He had a sense of humour, Olivia said, could laugh at himself. A reviewer wrote of the poet's impish humour, 'his spontaneity'; but what is kindness but another form of egotism, in some sly souls? Her time in Spain however had not been entirely wasted. She brought back some recipes. The recipe book was a lined notebook 6×4 with a marzipan design on the cover, crammed to bursting point with her impetuous scrawl, drawings of geese that laid golden eggs, a tureen on a long stand with protruding ladle suggestive of pleasing mouth-watering contents, the vertebrae of an upended fish.

CHAPTER XXIX

Before me, the Simian Hand: Lear

A short inclined intersection joins Fitzjohn's Avenue and Finchley Road. This was the short-cut you used when working for the priapic Persian. A small pagoda-style shelter of imitation marble stands on a land island at the upper entrance of College Crescent; the Crescent descends at an angled incline past the closed Tea Rooms and automobile salesrooms, coming out at the North Star Bar opposite the public baths at Swiss Cottage.

At a ground-floor window a simian hand drew aside the half-curtains and Oriental eyes studied you, a tall girl who knew a thing or two. You noticed a face smiling at you and made the mistake of smiling back. The curtains closed. Each morning you used the intersection, and came to notice him there working at his books and papers by the window. He was looking out for you. You passed there ten times a week, coming and going. Sometimes you came by the steps, passed the church of St. Thomas More, the former studio of old de Laszlo.

He came out for you.

You were caught on the land-island by traffic turning in eight different directions, and someone touched your arm. The Japanese student grinned from ear to ear, his narrow eyes just level with your chin. He excused himself, said he had noticed you coming and going to and from work. It was as if he knew you. He said his name. He came from Yokohama. You must excuse him, it was as if he knew you, a student like himself, the eldest son in a family of six, he had to work hard.

You told him you were from New Zealand.

Oh, he said, touching your arm; then we are practically neighbours. The classical approach, Olivia told me. He was a serious steady fellow, and did not go in for picking up girls off the street. Nor did you look like the sort of girl one picked up. I've seen you often, he said, noticed you . . . I believe I already know you.

The classical approach, Olivia said to me.

All week he studied, leaving himself no free time—only Saturday afternoons were free. Would you be his Saturday afternoon lover? His name: Lear Leer.

A black Rolls Royce went by, driven by a liveried chauffeur, in the back seat sat Ralph Richardson.

You will come next Saturday afternoon for lemon tea? the student Leer asked. He was sharply dressed in the dark pin-stripe suit with white shirt and pointed shoes. You will think about it seriously? He was studying Yeats. He had had tea with T. S. Eliot. Eliot had been amused at something he had said, and laughed. 'The esteemed author of "The Waste Land" laughs?' Oh, yes, Eliot had admitted, sometimes. Chink of teacups.

I might, you said, laughing at his persistence. I just might. 'And did you?' I asked.

Olivia rolled her hazel eyes at me.

After the Japanese there were others. Before Yokohama and after Yokohama; your life before me seemed to be full of admirers: Truss City, teeming with lechers. Peter Upward moved in with a plate of spaghetti, a pair of overheated Flamenco dancers swaggered from a darkened room with emission stains on their flies. After Major Angus Duncan McNair and the unknowns, after the Yokohama student and his spiked lemon tea, after the inverts and their flash bulbs, after the naked West Indian and the priapic Persian, Me. *Eau* desires communication, is indecisive, passive, evasive, intuitive and sensual, both compassionate and immoral at the same time (*'Poissons sans boisson est poison'*) weak before temptation, lightly touched by mysticism, open to drugs. Contradictions there.

173

Chris and Luther were two inverts from the flat below. They were good company, you said. They liked to talk to you in the bath, scrub your back. They photographed you, taken like a screen siren, glowing over one naked shoulder. Luther was so black he was almost blue. He said: 'Life is a rugged path that we try to make smude.' Chris could move his false teeth like a pike, taught art at Crouch End. They both confided in you. A third had died. You picked flowers on the heath, for the funeral, where a man exposed himself to you. Lonny's mother came from Natal, but her son was already dead. Lonny had played the piano, a gentle boy. He stood at the piano while you played. This was photographed too. It all took place in your room.

You were my unknown mistress. In you I had found both wife and mistress; rarely are both united in one person.

We watched the kite-fliers on Parliament Hill together ('Don't shout at your father, Joanna, it's *rewd*!'), drank in the King of Bohemia. You liked rum in winter, gin in summer. You had come over, burning with ambition, seeking a career on the London stage. Back home you had distinguished yourself in 'Sit Down a Minute, Adrian', a comedy by J. Brandon Thomas, which ran for three nights in aid of funds for the Red Cross ('a very creditable portrayal of the tragedy of love at 18'). Your mother, who still had good legs, sang 'Sweet Bird of Love Divine' at an open window. Your father, not on speaking terms with her, wrote in a hand as small and precise as Pepys'—the industrious Mr Pepys—in a neat law-abiding hand, the calligraphy of another century: *Debit*.

Sunset over vast landscapes and then the beginnings of hot nights, with trains shunting; squeal of metal getting into motion again, hiss of escaping steam. The Baptist bell ringing the small hours, the sound of cattle bellowing on their last night on earth. You had gone away. You were in London. You would never go home again. You wrote to them. They wrote to you.

Your career on the stage came to nothing.

An interview was arranged with John Gielgud. You did a read-through in a bar, a fiasco. Your stage career ended there and then. You threw away the script, began to work for the Persian. Then you worked for the Yugoslav Embassy in Holland Park. Randolph Churchill hired you as his personal secretary. Unshaven, uncombed, generally with a hangover, pacing to and fro, dictating. You went down flights of steps beyond the church of St. Thomas More. The Japanese student waited in vain.

Olivia went down four flights of stairs and came back unwrapping books she had ordered. 'The Plague' by Camus. I had never heard of it. I did not know Camus. Were you too clever for me?

You quoted:

      Since we are going to begin today
      Let us consider what it is you do.

CHAPTER XXX

The Icecream Factory

The icecream factory was vast: a brown windowless edifice somewhere beyond Willesden Junction. Trucks assembled in the yard at night in the heat-wave A tall shellshocked worker threw a fit in the canteen. At the loading bay a small coloured man went berserk, shouted 'Fuck your sister!' at a huge dull Irishman. He was given his walking-papers on the spot. The gates opened, a Black Maria pulled up, factory guards led him out, he walked away free. Tins jammed on the exits of the conveyor belt as the stuff poured out. The factory floor smelt of vomit. I worked in the freezing rooms for ten shillings a week extra, drawing good wages, exhausted all night, half-asleep on my feet. In the factory garden during the night break, exhausted black men in white overalls were laid out on the benches, as if headless and armless.

When the two heavy doors were opened, high up, an Arctic scene offered itself: snow and fog and the bays iced up. I sent the stuff out once, half-frozen. It was soft as shit. The ganger cursed me. Palsied with cold, I stopped the run, started another line, blowing into the iced up intercom. 'Try and stay awake, matey,' the ganger said.

Mick Swords of Tipperary caroused with friends in the West End, walking home to Shepherd's Bush after the last tube had gone. In Kensington Gardens a client copulated with a whore who drank from a bottle. Irish whores, Swords claimed, were the most inexpert ('dormant fucking rats').

Olivia was living with her friend Pat Godkens at Camden Hill. You asked what should you wear, skirt or slacks. Skirt. 'Oh?' We walked in Holland Park. White statuary was laid out on the grass of Holland House. The husband of Pat Godkens was a beast. Silence for the PM:

Eden on Suez. He drank double gins, overfed, overweight, glowering.

It was a sort of underground place reared up into the sky, spewing ice-cream and smelling of lost hopes and vomit. You came with me once to the gates; you were aghast, you really were. Do chaps work here? They really do. In the reassuring smell of old vomit.

CHAPTER XXXI

Tea with Mr Spender

'Porchester Terrace,' I told the taximan.

One could hear the bottle-party from the street. I went in. The host was nowhere to be seen. The lighting was dim in one room, the other completely dark, both crowded as jails.

Out of the darkened inner room presently came lean Flamenco dancers in tight black trousers, with cummerbands about their narrow waists, awash with sweat, their flies stained with emissions. They had been dancing with girls in the dark. They strutted in, gesticulating, showing the fillings in their teeth. A Mr Guy Tremlett and a My Roly Bagshot introduced themselves. Did I know Ryle and Jebb? No, really? Not know old Jebby, never heard of Binky? Their interest waned, was visibly dissipated. Dissolvent les éspoirs. They had no interest in the girls, now looking very flushed and tumbled, drinking wine out of cups. They had only eyes for the inflamed Flamenco dancers with the indecent stains. A right pair of whoresons. No drinks were offered. One brought one's own bottle.

'I'll snap it off!'

'Damn your yellow eyes!'

An Andalusian song began to whine on the hidden turntable and from the kitchen down the hall came host Peter Upward bearing a plate of spaghetti bolognaise, followed by a trim young thing carrying two mugs of wine. They sat back-to-back, Upward applying himself to the food. From the way he ignored her it was apparent that she was to be his that night.

'It was to be either Flamenco or booze,' Upward explained, wiping his lips with a tissue. 'We decided on Flamenco. Didn't we, kitten?'

Kitten rubbed her back against his. A tall girl in tartan slacks stood in a corner with two dull fellows.

'Jean—love!'

'Marty!' a strangled voice said. A mottled middle-aged man went by with a stunned girl in tow. She wore Italian sandals, a tight moss-green dress. The dancing girls in the darkened room sounded pissed as cunts. They were being tortured by the ferocious young Flamenco dancers.

'Who if I cried,' a cor anglais voice intoned, 'would hear me among the angelic orders?'

'Structure,' a thin voice articulated behind the sofa.

'May I?' I asked the green dress.

Couples circled the room in time to the gluey music issuing from the darkened inner room where the Flamenco dancers were having the time of their life. Their stamping feet sounded like hoofs. I danced close with the mottled man's girl, grasping her about the hips and girdle, moving slowly, now this way, now that, feeling her supple spine through the conducting agent of thigh and leg, floorboards.

'You'd never guess whom I had tea with last Tuesday,' she said, breathing Martini fumes into my face.

'Never,' I agreed.

'James Joyce,' she said. 'Don't hold me there please.'

'Don't quite get that.'

'No?'

'Absolutely no.'

'Oh but it's true,' she said, offering me a sweet lop-sided smile, and the honesty of her greenish eyes. I could smell her lipstick.

We circled slowly. I could smell the lipstick mixed with Martini. She was thinking.

'Not likely,' I said. 'No. Hardly possible. He's been dead since January 1941.'

We danced about. The room was hot and airless, buzzing with party-talk.

'Oh, I'm sorry,' she said, holding her head back,

watching my lips. 'I mean James Stephens. Last Tuesday I had tea with James Stephens.'

'I'd like to believe you.'

'You don't—why not?'

'He's dead too, unfortunately,' I said.

'Never heard that.'

We were hardly moving, cornered in a clot of dancers. Then it cleared a little, I steered her backwards, feeling her supple spine. The same Spanish song whined from the inner room. We danced around, the mottled man observing us.

'Oh but I am a fool,' the green girl whispered in my ear. 'It was Stephen Spender.'

'Much more likely,' I said. Considering.'

'Considering? Oh! Isn't *he* alive?'

'Absolutely,' I said. I could see the green girl taking tea with Mr Spender in tea-rooms near the British Museum. She showed him a notebook of handwritten poems. Spender bent forward. The music stopped. A fellow who had announced that he was in publishing asked the green girl for a dance. Rolling her eyes like a doll she was swept away.

'Structure,' a voice insisted. 'I do believe . . .'

'May I get you a drink?'

'Do forage around.'

I stood next to the mottled man, and soon was privy to unwanted confidences of an intimate nature. Most girls who went to bed with him conceived, he said, and all who did, brought forth daughters. But he couldn't make the green girl come.

'Come to bed?' I said.

'Have an orgasm.'

Perhaps it was his fault? he suggested. All those who conceived by him bore daughters. Middle-aged and thin on top, with teeth in ruins, they still wanted him, and he old enough to be their father. I heard his intestines rumbling, a blast of decay issued from his troubled interior along with unwanted confidences. His breath was foul.

'Can I take her home with me?' I asked.

The mottled man laughed. A tall girl with long black hair about a startling white face sailed by, very disdainful, in the arms of a fellow with double vents. They danced at arm's length, their teeth braced in hostility.

'Ivy Compton-Burnett,' an intense voice sang out. 'And Jack Yeets!'

A hand like a claw was laid on my shoulder.

'Know Shropshire?'

Know old Ryley? Know old Binks? No? The tall girl in tartan slacks was going home. The host was nowhere to be seen. He had taken the kitten away with him into a bedroom upstairs. The Flamenco dancers burst from the inner room, pointing long quivering fingers at each other and shouting 'Borachos! Boracho!'

Time to go home, Hanschen *Klein*. Time to go home.

CHAPTER XXXII

The Attic

The last Tube had certainly gone, sucked away into the foul-smelling tunnels, and the stations chained and padlocked for the night. Outside it would be cold; remote stars shone over Truss City. Narrow stairs smelling of dust led down. I could not tear myself from that warm attic.

'Stay if you like,' you said. 'There's a spare bed.' So I stayed, though not in the spare bed.

My own room stank like a larder, for I cooked and washed in the same room, slept there too; it was squeezed between high end-walls and cramped as a coffin. No sunlight could penetrate into Prince Edward Mansions. My landlady was French and believed that all the Irish were dirty in their habits. The place was a warren of admonitory notices, prohibitions of one sort or another. She looked for pubic hair in the bath. A drugged girl was sent weeping away. No questions were asked. In the near vicinity, two lobotomised patients, one a young woman, threw themselves from windows to their deaths. I lost my yale key down the stairwell. She opened the door resentfully in pink slippers and gown. The milk delivery came up in the lift. Movements late at night were frowned upon. In the daytime the thick carpet creaked; she was standing outside my door, breathing heavily, expecting the worst. The Irish were lazy too. An abject race. She was French. But I paid my rent on the nail, to Madame Sagaison.

So I stayed. It was the first night in Truss City with you, a city transformed. In the night it began to snow.

I walked a station platform under the city, numbed feeling the dead air of the trains blowing on my face and not minding. King's Cross Above ground it was still dark but below, in the murky heat, the early shift-workers were already heading for the factories. An obstinate crew, not young, set in their ways; their clothes the colour of mud.

A life of factory work, interrupted by war, perhaps a stint overseas, had worn them down. Then they had their country to serve but now they had only themselves, and they were lost, whether they knew it or not. They resembled, if it was anything living, old horses. Broken-winded work-horses, their usefulness at an end, ready for The Great Knacker.

I was with them in the deepest station, under the Zoo, Queen Mary's Gardens and the Toxophilite Society. They were bound for Northfields and Osterly, Fulham gas-works and the dreary stations to the West. Factory-darkened hands clutched Daily Mirrors and factory-fatigued eyes stared at the pin-up, the girl-for-the-day, a brunette pouting out more than her lips, with little on, well calculated to send the circulation up. Hers were the swelling haunches of a brood mare—a long shank of dark hair, thighs invoking stalls and hard-riding, hay: an expansive bosom was clamped into the twin cups of a minute bra. There was high summer in her gaze. Young, full, with parted lips, she stood provocative and near-nude on a hard coast, her extremities splashed by a cold sea, and suffered their impatient scrutiny, point by point. She was their lost summer, the one they had never enjoyed. In all that avid and packed repleteness, she was lending herself, giving herself over to the gross pleasures of exposure. The hot levelled gaze said 'Just you dare.' The cajoling poise: 'Try!' If the opened centre-spread was their morning feed-bag, she was their hay.

Reproduced twenty-thousand times, a hundred-thousand times, three million times, held fast in grimy fingers, breathed upon, stared at, devoured, enjoyed by proxy down there, down on the murky platforms under the city, the readers dizzy, nauseous, reeling from bed into this place where no air stirred but dead air, blown through the black tunnels by onrushing trains. The light flooded the carriage but it did not seem to belong to life proper. She was theirs for the morning, with that bold, dire look of hers, held fast breathed over, dreamed of, prized by famished eyes, stripped.

A beautiful blank face on a poster loomed up. I looked at bursting breasts pinched into the twin cups, one deep breath and nothing would hold. The air was not clean. The beautiful rapt face flew past, lights changed on a raised sign, the name WIMBLEDON lit up and hydraulic doors sprang open down the length of the train. I stepped into the grimy carriage and sat down opposite another corset advertisement. Tread the rubberised surface, grasp the moist pole! The doors clamped shut all together, half-opened again, then shut fast. The train shuddered down all its length and the platform began to flow past and the advertisements become blurred. I was flowing along towards Bromley and Upminister, Uxbridge, Hounslow West and its howling dogs. Lovely odd places no doubt, *Wurde, würde*, the train bored through the tunnels, pushing dead air before it, bearing me along the District Line.

I was travelling in the wrong direction. Nothing seemed to matter. It was a good joke. Misery was a joke. Even Rayners Lane. I was alive at last, sudden contact humming in me. Study the map, consult alternatives, go back, try again. Go on.

The cause of it slept away whatever remained of the night in her high attic. The covers of the spare bed were not disturbed. You said you would stand in the corner all night to frustrate generation, stop the baby. But you didn't. You lived high up and clean like a bird, there one could breathe. For me you represented freedom. Now that is strange, a delusion perhaps, but for the moment not. The W-shaped attic with its deep window embrasure was the secret house that a child might build in a tree.

'Could I come again?'

'Yes, if you wish.'

You wore a grey poloneck pullover and faded loose-fitting corduroys. Some friends had just left. You opened the window to clear the air, asked me to wait on the stairs while you changed. You changed into the bargee's outfit. I changed trains underground. The *Daily Mirror* girl looked like a rubber doll. I held onto another sweaty pole, sat on another worn seat, studied the same Tube map. Where are ye bound for, sad shufflers? Green, white and yellow, Waterloo and City lines, dirty white for Bank, brown for Bakerloo, black for the North. I found myself travelling backwards in elevated spirits on the yellow Circle Line, traversing the worn colours of the Irish flag. Bound now straight as a die for Hounslow and its maddened dogs. A carnival mood had taken hold. On I went, feeling nothing but compassion for those abject workers, bound for their several Limbos and Hells, always different and always the same.

Above, a day hard as iron was breaking. I breathed snow. It was snowing on Earls Court Road. Leaving behind the acid stinks of the cage, the touch of hard shoulders, I felt my shoes crunch on thin snow. The outlines of buildings loomed up, windows lit here and there. Office men and their secretaries were sleeping, waking perhaps twined together, for warmth. Two Indian girls in saris were laughing and trying to catch snowflakes in their open mouths. I went back to Prince Edward Mansions. To Flat No. 8, Moscow Road.

The milk delivery was already there. It had gone 8.00. Fired by new hopes I determined to work. Sleep for a few hours and then down to the studio in Notting Hill Gate in good order. I would take a bath, sleep a little and go down. I warmed a saucepan of milk over the gas-ring.

Evening. *Extase* at the Embassy. In a wood, near a Czech lake, Hedy Kreisler, Lemarr-to-be, removes her clothes; behind the leaves she is secret as a deer. Nude she is luminous. A single rain-drop moves down a window-pane, the ferrule of an umbrella crushes an insect crawling on a terrace, an old man's careful hand arranges objects on a bedside table, a hunch-backed groom brings bad news. She married an old man. It couldn't last. The bride gives herself to the woods, to the lake.

From the upper deck of a bus bound for Oxford Circus I saw a group of three on the pavement below. I recognised Jack Doyle the Horizontal Heavyweight from the old Tom Webster cartoons. Huggermuggering with a smart lady and a handler. Was the smart lady Movita? I did not recognise the sarong-clad island girl of the old 'Mutiny on the Bounty'. She was no longer young or ravishing. The boxer turned all-in-wrestler had the puffy features of the habitual heavy drinker. He wore an eye-patch. They seemed at a loss. The ex-boxer looking down. He still had curly black hair. They wanted to tear down Notting Hill Gate, level it to Shepherd's Bush.

At weekends now I was with you. I worked in the studio, living for the time we would be together. Soon I could not stay away from you. I took to coming during the week.

You walked in boots on the damp or freezing earth as if it pleased you. You liked the cold days, the last leaves dropping from the trees on the Heath, the kites straining over Parliament Hill Fields. Now you wore a white soft poloneck with tartan slacks.

'She has a really soiled face, that Jeanne Moreau,' you said. But I didn't understand you. There was nothing soiled about Jeanne Moreau's face. Perhaps it was the old man in you talking, airing prejudice? A Belgian umbrella manufacturer from Brussels had tried to get you drunk, force your to sit on his knee and say *'Je t'aime'*. He could not make you drunk. He wanted you to go to his hotel for a night. 'A big fat mercenary businessman—just imagine that!'

'I must have fruit,' you said, holding a ten shilling note in your gloved hand, prodding the cold fruit. To me it seemed extravagant. 'You have the palate of a dog.' Ever try avocado pears? Persimmons? Pawpaws? Ever eat yum-yums? The greengrocer beat his mittened hands together and told her that all his produce was fresh from Covent Garden. Puffing out his cheeks, he assured her his fruit and vegetables were first class. 'Aint got nothing bad here, Miss.'

You had nice hands, the wrists and arms too; such a shy smile, fragile. A fledgling, innocent, but hopeful. You were not prudish. 'Je ne regrette rien.'

You would not sit on the Belgian businessman's knee but you sat on Orson Welles's knee in a dream, looking at his lips, his sneering mouth. Meaning: a mouth capable of sneers. You thought he was mean. 'You are so mean,' you told Welles, 'it's coming out of your ears. Don't you feel it?' Welles jerked his head back, beckoned to someone behind him, opened his mouth 'like a cave', in order to say: 'Listen to this!' Throwing his head back he gave a rich expansive laugh. 'But he watches you craftily, to see how you take it. His eyes are curious.'

All your dreams were sexual. Perhaps I would appear in them one day. You were unusually nice, I thought, being easy and comfortable with your intelligence, though awkward in other ways; the awkwardness being only an added attraction.

'Must have fresh fruit.'

You disappeared down a hill carrying a Spanish basket. We sat under hunting prints in a pub. Touches of red, rat-catcher, raised vents, flushed faces, fleeing foxes. Did I know Gascoyne?

I frequently felt at a loss. Cooker of potatoes, cabbage, spaghetti bolognaise, in a room that stank, of cooking, of unwashed clothes, of discomfort, airless; I lived poorly.

'You must experiment. Open up.'

Gascoyne sat huddled next to you in a friend's car. You were driving down to Sussex to see George Barker.

Gascoyne said nothing all day, stood at Barker's door, took a noggin of Scotch from one pocket, handed it to Barker, took another noggin from the other pocket, went in without a word, and did not open his mouth all day except to drink, confining himself to making two remarks on the way home, pointing to a place where an underground river was reputed to flow, pointing to a field thought to be good for mushrooms. Mindful of the uncounted dead and how they outnumbered the living, he had stopped talking, thinking of all those dead ears listening. He had given up writing poetry and now painted pictures like Persian miniatures. He threatened to blow up Buckingham Palace.

Did I know Derain?

Her former boss had been a Persian ('Nothing miniature about him, though'), a handsome muscular man, most amorous. He had designs on her. The day began with him chasing her around the office. It was deadly serious. One day he arrived in the office with his flies open. "See what you have done to me, Orliffia Griff!' He was 'slung like a stallion'. The races continued. He was most persistent; and operating in something shady, munitions, arms deals. One set of files were top secret. He had the key. One day he phoned; she was to burn the secret files at once, the key was hidden in such a place. She was to admit nothing, the files never existed. It was a hot day. She had been sunbathing nude in the garden. An hour later he phoned to say it was a mistake. Too late, the files were destroyed. She was stark naked in the garden, raking up the charred remains, burying all evidence. He was hot and hasty, but not her lover, he never made it. One or two orgasms and an English girl was finished, he said. He had never had a New Zealand girl. 'Well, you can't begin with me, Haig Galustian.'

She shared a flat with two other Auckland girls, Georgina Wallace and Stephanie Briett, all good-lookers. A friendly West Indian sat naked on a rug before the fire, his skin so black it was almost blue. She was going out with a man from the Foreign Office. She had to lie naked on the bed and say 'I want to be focked.' English lust, Olivia said, colonial expansion, kinks; Daw of the FO was difficult to please, he was one of those. He took taxis everywhere. A taxi, a rickshaw, an obliging houri girl, Chepstow Villas. He was cruel. She was an innocent. He was her first, this overbearing Daw. He swung from the ceiling, he was Icarus, Prometheus, a vulture; she was his slave, his food, he was intolerable.

One other fellow intervened, of those worthy of mention in the roster of her admirers. A tall shy fellow who painted fish. He took her to concerts. Olivia armoured herself in a black corset to go out with the painter of fish, since music meant nothing to me. She came back alone in a taxi. She had not been able to eat, threw up in the loo. 'I was thinking of you.'

We sat again under the running foxes, the touches of red, the ruddy-faced huntsmen, my money drained away. 'It doesn't matter,' you said. 'We don't need much money.' You knew a place where greens were cheaper. I searched in Islington for a lost earring. In Collins's Music Hall a stripper was pushed naked on a bicycle across the stage. Pauline ('Take 'em Off') Penny wore a seraphic smile, but nothing else. I never found the lost earring. You tended to loose things, Olivia. You really did.

You armoured yourself in a black French corset, made up your eyes. Daw and the Persian had disappeared. The tall serious man who painted only fish, ate only fish, had come to live in the flat below. The place stank of fish fries. He was a poor painter. You laughed at the nude cyclist.

Leaning perilously out the attic window you called down four stories to the milk roundsman. You were naked from the waist down. 'Milkman!' you called in an English-Scots accent. You wanted Gold Top Cream. I lay between blue sheets and marvelled at you. I had bought a second-hand wedding-ring in Kentish Town. One of the bed-legs was broken, broken before my time, and now supported by half a brick. Dressed in a peony-red dressing gown you brought breakfast on a tray. You had a dream. Sitting cross-legged on the bed, with a towel wound about your wet hair like a turban, you told me your dream. You were a boy. You fondled your mother's breasts. Then you were in a street. A very pretty girl stopped and stared at you. She said, 'Well, I suppose there's nothing for it but to retire upstairs.' You were a boy. You came to a building, entered a lift, the girl pressed the button, the lift began to ascend. You faced each other but not touching, smiling. When the lift stopped the dream ended. What did it mean? Under certain circumstances a smile can be as good as a promise. You removed the tray, then the dressing gown. 'Make me warm,' you said and got into bed with me.

'The nicest feeling,' you admitted, 'waking up in the wrong end of town, strange territory, coming home in a taxi.' Where we were was home. Home is where one sets off from. Your life before me seemed full of admirers. Roy Earlham was phoning HAM 8348. So was Nirodi Nazunda. Vuck Eisen, home-sick for Yugoslavia, called. A strikingly handsome man. He was studying to be a surgeon. They phoned or were hovering about.

An unknown mistress possesses a unique charm. But while the charm of novelty yields progressively to the knowledge of character, perfectly pure pleasure comes only with intimacy. At first it's victory; in the following you acquire intimacy. Afterwards comes pure felicity, provided one is dealing with an intelligent woman. Extase.

Were you too intelligent for me, answering HAM 8348, travelling on the 187 out of Pond Street, taking the Number 31 to Kensington High Street through the poplar blossoms that were blowing from Holland Park, leaving the bus to go on to World's End? Were you, my dearest?

CHAPTER XXXIII

Life at Gospel Oak

Then we moved.

Olivia from Belsize Lane and I from Prince Edward Mansions in Notting Hill Gate, to be closer to her at Buckland Crescent in Swiss Cottage (a single narrow high-ceilinged room with the bust of a surly Roman head in one corner, a small balcony overlooking the crescent, where Pakistani and Indian families were beginning to move in. I painted rubber Scotsmen four inches high for a film publicity stunt, at 2/6d. each. The room overflowed with tiny Highlanders in kilts, they were on the chair, in the bed. ('Get rid of those bloody Scotsmen,' Olivia begged); and then both of us together to Gospel Oak where I had the use of a house at Number 2 Elaine Grove, a run-down address in a short street that no taximan could ever find, until the place was pulled down or the owner returned.

The house was small, the rooms cramped, damp all winter and dusty all summer, a domicile fit for dwarfs. Once it had been a grocer's shop. I covered the wide window of the front room with a sheet and worked there relatively undisturbed. Children played in the street outside. It would do. The man who paid the rent was in Castagniers; a painter. The place was ours until his return. There was a pub adjacent, the Pig and Garter. My wife spent much time there reading Hardy; she was deep into Wessex.

In the back yard I rigged up a primitive shower under an awning. Olivia closed her eyes, catching her breath under the sudden shock of cold that made her nipples erect, while on her bush the drops sparkled, now calling for the jet to be weaker, now stronger, her diaphragm heaving and the water streaming off her. I painted her nude, sleeping in the awning now converted into a hammock, one long thoroughbred thigh flung out. The shadows of chestnut leaves on taut canvas (the buds thick and sticky, the splayed leaves heavy, dust-laden), her young outline braced against the damp, her winter paleness going. At night we swam in the Women's Pool on the Heath, I covered her with blossoms, lay on her. Her lips tasted of fruit, resinous juices. Her past, obscure enough, had become more real than my own. Members of eccentric religious sects came floundering down the hill, arms spread wide, calling out incomprehensible incantations.

She lay in lukewarm water in the cracked tub and let me use pumice stone on her long ingenue's legs. When I shaved her with my razor and contrived to nick her, she lay on her stomach in the bloodstained water cursing my awkwardness as I soaped her fore and aft, her meadow-brown hair bound into two braids and tied with red rubber bands. Her viands were most exquisitely farced.

Then, glowingly, stepping from the bath and letting the water drain away, she began drying herself so that I could oil her, the ritual oiling, with towel about her hips accentuating the length of her body, and presently catch me admiring all this in the mirror, and roll her hips so that the towel fell, sketch a shimmy, and saunter out of the drenched bathroom, a nervy beauty. In the peony-red dressing gown she might eat an apple, read Hardy, as naked under her gown as that lady of old Verona who went out, to offer herself, nude under her cloak, to the commander of the beseiging army. By this sacrifice she intended to save Verona.

When you stood, diminished under the giantesses painted by Paolo Veronese (the most flittering light of old Parma's School) in the National Gallery in Trafalgar Square, under that huge and torpid sprawl of brownskinned lethargic propagators, whose oaken-coloured limbs were as the branches of great oaks, whose breedy trunks were their most substantial boles, whose well-fleshed haunches had the commanding girth of great groaning branches, whose hair was the colour of beech-leaves in autumn, whose opthalmic eyes, as if stunned or drugged, stared from the boscage, high up, not to be seen or identified—what did I think of then but of an unimaginable daughter whom I had never seen (because yet unborn) and what I would call her.

Pola, Pilar, Alva, Asta, Inez, Viva, Vita, Norinà, Dorothy, Dora, Penelope, Dorothea, Ursula, Abigail, Fatima, Katja, Minna, Tania, Merloyd, Elaine, Eva, Vera, Ita, Tina, Yara, Vivi, Yvette, Honoré, Sophie, Veronica, Saniette, Merlaine, Veronique, Rosina, Binetta, Varna, Josephine (Beppa), Paula, Erica, Elaina, Seraphina, Lunia, Salina, Edelgunda, Sayalonga, Beatrice (Bea), Selraggia, Hippolita, Andromeda, Celia, Carla, Virginia, Messalina, Marguerita, Yara, Camilla, Goya, Flora, Oona, Zamira, Mashenka, Diomeda, Cornella, Devorgilla, Cordelia, Johanna, Felicita, Nadia, Marcia, Moydia, Djuna, Wanda, Renata, Pina, Gemma, Barbara.,Francesca, Fiona, Melanie, Margot, Maria, Marriane, Mirabel, Monique, Sabina, Isabella, Clytemnestra, Ariadne, Apasia, Iphigenia, Poppoea, Petrushka, Diana, Vesta, Hetta, Binetta, Minerva, Livia, Esther, Nadine, Undine, Demeter, Dympna, Emmanuela, Roxana, Judith, Margaret, Bathsheba, Dulcima, Laurentia, Amestis, Persephone, Althea, Numa, Electra, Etricia, Patricia, Lydia, Anna, Rena, Renata, Rosita, Nina, Nanna, Ada, Annabella, Augusta, Elmira, Clare, Nell, Madeleine, Freya, Lolette, Lorna, Ina, Mina, Fanny, Juanita, Alice, Eavan, Helene, Rose, Molly, Harriet, Hannelore, Philomena, Anne-Marie, Brigid, Betty, Susan, Alma, Evelyn, Karin, Hilda, Nora, Moira, Stella, Berenice, Linda, Sylvia, Hanna, Misha, Angela, Tamara and Mia.

Ruttle was a hard name to match. Karin Ruttle? Elaine Ruttle.

When she was born he was already an old man, set in his ways, a notary, a family lawyer who made out deeds of possession in a minute script. He sucked little black pastiles, wore a wing collar, a choker, button boots, spread pipe tobacco to dry on his desk and shouted at his clients. Deaf as a post but vain, he would not use a hearing-aid or ear-trumpet; all his life he had worked hard, putting in eight and ten hours a day at the age of fifty as he would at ninety, still in harness, still shouting at his clients. They were obliged to shout back, all manner of indiscretions. He was her beloved Pop, the best Pop in the whole wide world. And she was his one and only Billy. 'Done your home-work Billy? Been to the dubs Billy? Don't be late Billy.'

Her mother called her Shell, gave little indication of affection, much less love. 'My girl.' Olivia dropped things.

We sat on a wooden public bench on the hill in the sun and watched the kites flying. Below Parliament Hill Fields the ground fell away to the ponds, willows and poplar below the copper beech.

'Pop had me too late,' Olivia said. 'He'd turned forty the year I was born. It was too late. Anyway he wanted another boy.'

A small Oriental flew a ferocious dragon, twenty feet long, if not longer, all teeth and glaring eyes. The red and black dragon-body, glistening as if covered in blood, went wobbling and jerking up over the trees. The dragon swelled as it filled with wind, as its owner, running backwards whilst unreeling, shrank away to nothing.

'It's too late,' Olivia said, watching the ascending red dragon.

'Too late for what?'

'To be a father,' Olivia said, smiling at the antics of the dragon, 'at forty.'

'Tush tush. Not in Ireland. At least not in the old days.'

'For God's sake,' Olivia said, 'look at the Irish!'

'True.'

Now the dragon was far up, and still rising, its owner calmly unreeling line that curved away from him, up and up.

'If I could paint,' Olivia said, 'if I could, I'd paint those kids. Look at them jump. You can see the sky under their feet. In Ireland they'd be stuck to the ground. Up to their knees. You couldn't separate them.'

We had taken to going by Willow Walk onto Parliament Hill Fields and across the Heath to Highgate village, down a step into the old Flask where Hogarth had once caroused, sitting snug with a covey of wags.

We passed Gaels with scorched faces and stringy white legs, engaged in hurley, wearing mismatched colours and stockings rolled down to the ankles. Some wore crash helmets, all were roaring out the Holy Name as they whirled and struck in a froth of excitement, the dun-coloured ball soaring in a long arc down the uneven field. They were back in Tipperary, in Kerry, in woody Kildare.

'Now Tom Malone!'

'Now Tom avic!'

Tom Malone was in a class of his own, with white hair, a green jersey.

'Up Down!' Olivia said. 'Every time.'

The sun was sinking. Truss City had disappeared. It was just a glow over the horizon. They were all back in Tipperary, they had never left it. They had changed under an oak tree. Now they were struggling near one of the goals, a pile of coats. The hurley sticks smacked fiercely together.

'Oh Jaysus you ejit!'

'Blood will be spilt,' Olivia said.

CHAPTER XXXIV

The Pond

High hoardings advertised beer and lager at Mornington Crescent, a name suggestive of a brightness that was not there. Two young lethargic late-rising whores exercised French poodles in Queensway. Stone statues of immense cats sat on their tails outside the Carreras factory. A whistle was blowing. Crowds of the damned walked by the National Temperance Hospital. A brownstone church of unknown denomination had its gates permanently closed; above it a skyline that cramped the heart.

Opposite the underground WC Fortress Road stood a toy-shop that went in for wooden Russian toys. We were happy then, Olivia and I, in a drugged fashion. In the neighbourhood of Camden Town I bought a great second-hand trunk. The shop-owner threw it onto the pavement to show how it could take hard knocks. I had sold some paintings. We were saving for an Adriatic voyage.

I lay on the moored raft and watched the white blossoms drifting off the poplar trees that grew around Hampstead Pond. Through slitted eyes, the stagnant brown water resembled a river. The causeway was a bridge. Serious men fished there with gaffs and waders as if after salmon in a running stream. When a swimmer dived from the raft or another gained it, it tipped and brown water washed over it. But now I was alone on it. An odour difficult to describe rose from the bed of the disturbed pond. Girls in tight costumes swam in the dirty water, breast-stroking, holding their heads high. The Regius Professor was among them, something foul (snot or emission) caught in the forks of his Mandarin beard. I closed my eyes. The sun was hot. The raft began to tilt. I opened my eyes. A plump girl in a yellow costume was hauling herself aboard. She had left a wake of scent in the water, now it was on the raft.

The sun shone on the sun-bathers. It was a hot summer. Poplar blossoms drifted by in the breeze, as though the pond-water was moving. The plump girl stretched herself out on the damp boards. She lay there calm as a leaf, caught in a fluid sensual dream. Her diaphragm heaved mightily. A rowing-boat was putting out from the bathing-place, the little lido among the trees. At the end of the wooden jetty, the sunbather who had been immersed in 'Malone meurt' sat with his feet submerged in the water, staring down; his extremities appeared to be severed below the knees. The oarsman pulled easily. As the boat approached I saw that he, without any distinctness, resembled Ussher.

Her dreams were sexual: the dream of furniture being washed ashore on a beach, real antiques; the dream of the match-box that contained Field Marshal Montgomery, a little figure that rolled its eyes when you tilted the match-box; then the real Field Marshal stood on a mound nearby, looking over her head; under his arm he carried rolled maps. Soon I too would be there, in her dreams.

When she put down the breakfast tray, her covering fell off. She climbed into bed with me. 'Make me warm.' Her life before me was full of admirers, those threatening phantoms, Persians and Chinamen, a Yugoslav, an Indian. She lay on her stomach in bloodstained water, my Lady of Verona.

In the dingy perlieus of Camden Town I'd bought a second-hand trunk the size of a wardrobe, weathered oxidized green as if removed from water. The shopman, dingy as his premises, heaved it onto the pavement. I had some trouble getting it aboard a bus. Crusoe lugging his painted chest across the Ox Mountains. Passengers had to force their way past it. For our Adriatic voyage. I had sold three paintings, bought the second-hand gold wedding-ring in Kentish Town. We were on our way.

A little brown-faced man was walking in a shower of rain, moving on a shining pavement as if walking on water, umbrella raised above a curly-brim derby hat safe inside plastic, smiling to himself. Impassive Egyptian stone cats, drugged on curare, sat outside the Carreras factory. 'Orpheé' was showing at the Berkeley. A brownstone church of unknown denomination had its doors permanently closed, the outside gate padlocked. Around there, under the hoardings, the damned were walking under a skyline that might well cramp the heart. I did not recognise the tall girl dressed in red crossing the ramp with towel and bathing costume in a basket. It was Olivia.

My wife walked by the copse of trees next to the church on Rosyln Hill, carrying a string bag full of groceries. Living with her, the smells were different, rooms were aired, carpets brushed, flowers in vases. I began to have regular meals. It was the first hot summer, the first and last hot summer there.

We are in the chilly water and the sun has gone down. All around us the scum, the spent blossoms. The raft is empty. We are the last. Among the saplings emerging from the water around the pond the poplar blossoms are trapped in scummy foam. The boatman who resembles both the dead Cavé and the living Ussher watches us. He has a weather-beaten face, long countryman's cheeks, and smokes a pipe. Noble it is to decay growing wise, as metaphysics wears out the heart.

We are in a bus. Pedestrians dressed in muddy colours hurry along Tottenham Court Road and disappear into the bowels of the earth by Goodge Street tube entrance. On huge hoardings raised above the traffic ideally healthy couples bare their teeth to the gums. A salesgirl home-sick for the Antipodes vomits up something that resembles an ostrich egg, but green, in the basement of Heal's. Harried shoppers gape at window displays, kitchen appliances, bedroom fittings, toys for tots, infant baths. I am thinking of a daughter and what I might call her: Katja. Olivia is greatly pregnant. It has not improved her temper. She is 'off' smoking and drinking, and suffering from morning sickness, reading 'Jude the Obscure'.

Gaunt effigies of monumental stone cats, certainly Egyptian in origin, lean as lynxes, fifteen feet high and resting on their haunches, guard the entrance to the Carreras factory. The cat is very dear to Ham, who was the first painter: Narcissus. A man shell-shocked in the Great War points a Service revolver at his red-headed grown son, consorting with a whore. The revolver is not loaded, the whore is not abed. Angry words are exchanged in the little yardway. Crowds of the damned pass.

Olivia walking home with celery, avocado pears, mandarin oranges. We were happy in a drugged manner, supposing Pisces and Balance can be happy together. It was the beginning.

Now in Oxo-coloured water I am holding you, lifting you above the scum, the mire, and you are laughing. Laughter comes so naturally out of you, child-like, hopeful. We are in the shadows. No matter. In the chilly water. As I sink, you rise, held up by the waist. Aloft in the air you are laughing. My head is below the surface. I can feel your laughter in my hands, as if it were the best joke in the world. The world gone from us. We are slipping away. All around us the scum, the spent blossoms floating over the dark Oxo-coloured water. The raft is empty. We are the last.

Was it not like that in those near-perfect autumn days, when I was again, after I had thought all that was finished, routed by something afar?

Somewhere a whistle was blowing. Someone was playing a piano in Well Walk. You had begun smoking and drinking again, morning sickness had passed off. We drank gin in The King of Bohemia. Reading Hardy, looking down the valley towards the trees. In the deep cover we were hidden away. We were weak in the bones, from touching. Was it like that on Box Hill?

The raft tilts. On the wooden jetty a stone's throw away, the cadaverous reader stares aghast at his immersed extremities, cut off just below the knee. The sun shines on sticky sun-bathers, oiled and creamed, a rowing-boat is pulling out from behind the wooden jetty. The oarsman pulls easily, taking his time, not disturbing the swimmers or the water-fowl. As he comes on I see that he strangely resembles Ussher who resembles the dead Cavé, the friend of Degas. The boat leaves a line of bubbles behind it. High up in the azure an unseen jet fighter bangs through the sound-barrier and more blossoms, as though there were some connection, are shaken from the poplars that line the pond. Turning in mid-pond and shipping his oars, Ussher-Cavé now begins retrieving something with a grappling hook. Do as I tell you and you will find out my shape. There are no pure substances in nature. Each is contained in each. A philosopher without any philosophy is retrieving an un-identified object from dark scummy water with a grappling hook.

I lie there letting time drift. Impressions offer themselves, focus, slip away. The raft rocks again. Brown water washes over it. The plump girl, heavy as a stove, has dived off. Her scent lingers, sweetly cloying, not pleasant. The Regius Professor is going back, breast-stroking calmly through filth. A tall auburn-haired beauty in a red dress is crossing the causeway with a towel under her arm.

I leave the raft, letting the water receive me. It is not only filthy but tepid, both bidet and toilet, the used bathwater of thousands. The blossoms are scum. As I touch the jetty, Olivia appears above me, adjusting her bathing-cap. Her face has changed with the hair hidden. She leans forward, poised to dive. The boatman is examining the dripping object. Olivia launches herself from the jetty above me.

CHAPTER XXXV

Baboushka-Katinka

In the toy-shop by the underground toilets the toys are made of wood from Soviet forests. A wooden Katinka-Baboushka stands corpulently on a wooden base, Soviet chickens pick on a circular wooden base. I pick up the Katinka-Baboushka. Unscrew the middle and discover within another peasant woman just as rotund. Unscrew her by the middle and discover another yet within. And within her another. Unscrew again to discover the smallest of all. Expressions range from the complacent to the guarded and resigned. The last little figure seemed far off, even when held in the hand, not only expressionless but featureless, standing as if resigned to it, rigid with—could it be fear? She has a blank bitter face.

Baboushka-Katinka must have been an unlucky omen, a Soviet jinx. For in the second week of her fifth month, my poor wife lost her child, my daughter. The toy was unlucky. I had bought it and hidden it away as a surprise present for our unborn daughter.

The rotund peasantry wore no convivial expression but something other, convulsed and thickly congested. They had lapsed from normal stoutness into lumpishness, ele-phantitis, into outlandish and surely painful proportions. I held the accursed object in my hand, shook it, took it out and burnt it, expecting worms to come from it.

Now Olivia is thin again. She is drinking and smoking and engaging in other pursuits just as before, but not reading Hardy in The Pig and Garter. She sits in the damp bedroom for hours on end. And now there is serious talk that No. 2 will have to come down. Our Adriatic tickets are booked. Olivia needs a change. Truss City is collapsing.

We are in a taxi, homeward bound. I have the tickets. The green sea-chest is packed.

'Elaine Grieve,' I tell the taximan.

'Idiot,' Olivia said.

'Alright,' I said, 'alright. Take us home. Elaine Grove.'

Then began the run-around. We were whirled through the unbright Mornington Crescent, over into Kentish Town where I had bought some woman's discarded wedding-ring and inherited her bad luck, through Chalk Farm into Swiss Cottage, from thence into Camden Town again, and across Delancey Street of all places, over a railway bridge, passing in and out of depressed areas of Gospel Oak, and from thence into regions of Truss City that I had never seen before or ever want to see again. The taximan was cursing and consulting a street map. I watched his neck, observing the numerals changing for the different Boroughs, the digits scrambling on the meter, racing on the clock. Home. Would we ever find it again?

CHAPTER XXXVI

Adriatic-Aegean

Supposedly, then, one day, a day like today, a day like any other day, a train would take us to Dover. Friends might see us off. Passing through the Vale of Kent and its orchards we would reach the Channel. At Ostende another train would be waiting. Young Germans might call out to Olivia, invite her into their carriage. Come with us to Berlin. The train would take us into Germany, that strange country. Change in the middle of the night for Köln. Rijeka early next morning.

The old address no longer existed now. No. 2 Elaine Grove has been pulled down. Pinker had returned to Canada.

One morning I would sit in a deckchair in the sun. The prow of the coastal steamer would cut through the Adriatic with hardly a sound. The Dinaric Alps, a mountain of ashes. At six in the morning—Dubrovnik. I would sleep on deck. Ahead lay Greece, another life. Would it be like that?

Forwarding address;

Hotel Supetar,
Mlini, Dalmatia,
Yugoslavia

or;

Od. Heracliton 191
Kolonaki,
Greece.

Take your pick.

CHAPTER XXXVII

End

Rain was pouring down, our taxi ploughed through it.
Olivia held onto the strap as Delancey Street flew by again.
We were knocked together, cold as clams. Nothing helped.

Dead brother Emmett had once attempted to teach
his sister mathematics. A total failure. You can take 1
away from 2 but where is it? He said, it still exists
somewhere in some form or another. (Nothing ever disappears. Nothing he said or did could surprise her; she
expected that of him. But this made no sense to her). He
always surprised her. 'Let x equal *what?*' you asked. 'It makes
no sense at all to me.'

It made no sense to me.

The taxi carried us on through the murk, the encircling
gloom, the driver apparently lost. Somewhere a ship was
waiting.

We were passing through broken-down Kentish Town.
Hold onto nothing; nothing lasts.

Long ago I was this, was that, twisting and turning,
incredulous, baffled, believing nothing, believing all. Now I
am, what? I feel frightened, sometimes, but may be just
tired. I feel depressed quite often, but may be just hungry.

All but blind
In his chambered hole
Gropes for worms . . .

ETROS ABATZOGLOU, *What Does Mrs. Freeman Want?*
IERRE ALBERT-BIROT, *Grabinoulor.*
UZ ALESHKOVSKY, *Kangaroo.*
VETLANA ALEXIEVICH, *Voices from Chernobyl.*
ELIPE ALFAU, *Chromos.*
    Locos.
VAN ÂNGELO, *The Celebration.*
    The Tower of Glass.
AVID ANTIN, *Talking.*
JUNA BARNES, *Ladies Almanack.*
    Ryder.
OHN BARTH, *LETTERS.*
    Sabbatical.
VETISLAV BASARA, *Chinese Letter.*
NDREI BITOV, *Pushkin House.*
OUIS PAUL BOON, *Chapel Road.*
OGER BOYLAN, *Killoyle.*
IGNÁCIO DE LOYOLA BRANDÃO, *Zero.*
HRISTINE BROOKE-ROSE, *Amalgamemnon.*
RIGID BROPHY, *In Transit.*
IEREDITH BROSNAN, *Mr. Dynamite.*
ERALD L. BRUNS,
    Modern Poetry and the Idea of Language.
ABRIELLE BURTON, *Heartbreak Hotel.*
IICHEL BUTOR, *Degrees.*
    Mobile.
    Portrait of the Artist as a Young Ape.
. CABRERA INFANTE, *Infante's Inferno.*
    Three Trapped Tigers.
ULIETA CAMPOS, *The Fear of Losing Eurydice.*
NNE CARSON, *Eros the Bittersweet.*
AMILO JOSÉ CELA, *The Family of Pascual Duarte.*
    The Hive.
OUIS-FERDINAND CÉLINE, *Castle to Castle.*
    London Bridge.
    North.
    Rigadoon.
IUGO CHARTERIS, *The Tide Is Right.*
EROME CHARYN, *The Tar Baby.*
IARC CHOLODENKO, *Mordechai Schamz.*
MILY HOLMES COLEMAN, *The Shutter of Snow.*
OBERT COOVER, *A Night at the Movies.*
TANLEY CRAWFORD, *Some Instructions to My Wife.*
OBERT CREELEY, *Collected Prose.*
ENÉ CREVEL, *Putting My Foot in It.*
ALPH CUSACK, *Cadenza.*
USAN DAITCH, *L.C.*
    Storytown.
IGEL DENNIS, *Cards of Identity.*
ETER DIMOCK,
    A Short Rhetoric for Leaving the Family.
RIEL DORFMAN, *Konfidenz.*
OLEMAN DOWELL, *The Houses of Children.*
    Island People.
    Too Much Flesh and Jabez.
IKKI DUCORNET, *The Complete Butcher's Tales.*
    The Fountains of Neptune.
    The Jade Cabinet.
    Phosphor in Dreamland.
    The Stain.
    The Word "Desire."
VILLIAM EASTLAKE, *The Bamboo Bed.*
    Castle Keep.
    Lyric of the Circle Heart.
EAN ECHENOZ, *Chopin's Move.*
TANLEY ELKIN, *A Bad Man.*
    Boswell: A Modern Comedy.
    Criers and Kibitzers, Kibitzers and Criers.
    The Dick Gibson Show.
    The Franchiser.
    George Mills.

    The Living End.
    The MacGuffin.
    The Magic Kingdom.
    Mrs. Ted Bliss.
    The Rabbi of Lud.
    Van Gogh's Room at Arles.
ANNIE ERNAUX, *Cleaned Out.*
LAUREN FAIRBANKS, *Muzzle Thyself.*
    Sister Carrie.
LESLIE A. FIEDLER,
    Love and Death in the American Novel.
GUSTAVE FLAUBERT, *Bouvard and Pécuchet.*
FORD MADOX FORD, *The March of Literature.*
CARLOS FUENTES, *Terra Nostra.*
    Where the Air Is Clear.
JANICE GALLOWAY, *Foreign Parts.*
    The Trick Is to Keep Breathing.
WILLIAM H. GASS, *The Tunnel.*
    Willie Masters' Lonesome Wife.
ETIENNE GILSON, *The Arts of the Beautiful.*
    Forms and Substances in the Arts.
C. S. GISCOMBE, *Giscome Road.*
    Here.
DOUGLAS GLOVER, *Bad News of the Heart.*
KAREN ELIZABETH GORDON, *The Red Shoes.*
GEORGI GOSPODINOV, *Natural Novel.*
PATRICK GRAINVILLE, *The Cave of Heaven.*
HENRY GREEN, *Blindness.*
    Concluding.
    Doting.
    Nothing.
JIŘÍ GRUŠA, *The Questionnaire.*
JOHN HAWKES, *Whistlejacket.*
AIDAN HIGGINS, *A Bestiary.*
    Flotsam and Jetsam.
    Langrishe, Go Down.
    Scenes from a Receding Past.
    Windy Arbours.
ALDOUS HUXLEY, *Antic Hay.*
    Crome Yellow.
    Point Counter Point.
    Those Barren Leaves.
    Time Must Have a Stop.
MIKHAIL IOSSEL AND JEFF PARKER, EDS., *Amerika:*
    Contemporary Russians View the United States.
GERT JONKE, *Geometric Regional Novel.*
JACQUES JOUET, *Mountain R.*
HUGH KENNER, *Flaubert, Joyce and Beckett:*
    The Stoic Comedians.
DANILO KIŠ, *Garden, Ashes.*
    A Tomb for Boris Davidovich.
TADEUSZ KONWICKI, *A Minor Apocalypse.*
    The Polish Complex.
ELAINE KRAF, *The Princess of 72nd Street.*
JIM KRUSOE, *Iceland.*
EWA KURYLUK, *Century 21.*
VIOLETTE LEDUC, *La Bâtarde.*
DEBORAH LEVY, *Billy and Girl.*
    Pillow Talk in Europe and Other Places.
JOSÉ LEZAMA LIMA, *Paradiso.*
OSMAN LINS, *Avalovara.*
    The Queen of the Prisons of Greece.
ALF MAC LOCHLAINN, *The Corpus in the Library.*
    Out of Focus.
RON LOEWINSOHN, *Magnetic Field(s).*
D. KEITH MANO, *Take Five.*
BEN MARCUS, *The Age of Wire and String.*
WALLACE MARKFIELD, *Teitlebaum's Window.*
    To an Early Grave.
DAVID MARKSON, *Reader's Block.*
    Springer's Progress.
    Wittgenstein's Mistress.

FOR A FULL LIST OF PUBLICATIONS, VISIT:
www.dalkeyarchive.com

SELECTED DALKEY ARCHIVE PAPERBACKS

CAROLE MASO, *AVA.*
LADISLAV MATEJKA AND KRYSTYNA POMORSKA, EDS.,
    *Readings in Russian Poetics: Formalist and
        Structuralist Views.*
HARRY MATHEWS,
    The Case of the Persevering Maltese: Collected Essays.
    Cigarettes.
    The Conversions.
    The Human Country: New and Collected Stories.
    The Journalist.
    My Life in CIA.
    Singular Pleasures.
    The Sinking of the Odradek Stadium.
    Tlooth.
    20 Lines a Day.
ROBERT L. MCLAUGHLIN, ED.,
    *Innovations: An Anthology of Modern &
        Contemporary Fiction.*
STEVEN MILLHAUSER, *The Barnum Museum.*
    In the Penny Arcade.
RALPH J. MILLS, JR., *Essays on Poetry.*
OLIVE MOORE, *Spleen.*
NICHOLAS MOSLEY, *Accident.*
    Assassins.
    Catastrophe Practice.
    Children of Darkness and Light.
    The Hesperides Tree.
    Hopeful Monsters.
    Imago Bird.
    Impossible Object.
    Inventing God.
    Judith.
    Natalie Natalia.
    Serpent.
    The Uses of Slime Mould: Essays of Four Decades.
WARREN F. MOTTE, JR.,
    Fables of the Novel: French Fiction since 1990.
    Oulipo: A Primer of Potential Literature.
YVES NAVARRE, *Our Share of Time.*
DOROTHY NELSON, *Tar and Feathers.*
WILFRIDO D. NOLLEDO, *But for the Lovers.*
FLANN O'BRIEN, *At Swim-Two-Birds.*
    At War.
    The Best of Myles.
    The Dalkey Archive.
    Further Cuttings.
    The Hard Life.
    The Poor Mouth.
    The Third Policeman.
CLAUDE OLLIER, *The Mise-en-Scène.*
FATRIK OUŘEDNÍK, *Europeana.*
FERNANDO DEL PASO, *Palinuro of Mexico.*
ROBERT PINGET, *The Inquisitory.*
    Mahu or The Material.
RAYMOND QUENEAU, *The Last Days.*
    Odile.
    Pierrot Mon Ami.
    Saint Glinglin.
ANN QUIN, *Berg.*
    Passages.
    Three.
    Tripticks.
ISHMAEL REED, *The Free-Lance Pallbearers.*
    The Last Days of Louisiana Red.
    Reckless Eyeballing.
    The Terrible Threes.
    The Terrible Twos.
    Yellow Back Radio Broke-Down.
JULIÁN RÍOS, *Larva: A Midsummer Night's Babel.*
    Poundemonium.

AUGUSTO ROA BASTOS, *I the Supreme.*
JACQUES ROUBAUD, *The Great Fire of London.*
    Hortense in Exile.
    Hortense Is Abducted.
    The Plurality of Worlds of Lewis.
    The Princess Hoppy.
    Some Thing Black.
LEON S. ROUDIEZ, *French Fiction Revisited.*
VEDRANA RUDAN, *Night.*
LYDIE SALVAYRE, *The Lecture.*
LUIS RAFAEL SÁNCHEZ, *Macho Camacho's Beat.*
SEVERO SARDUY, *Cobra & Maitreya.*
NATHALIE SARRAUTE, *Do You Hear Them?*
    Martereau.
ARNO SCHMIDT, *Collected Stories.*
    Nobodaddy's Children.
CHRISTINE SCHÜTT, *Nightwork.*
GAIL SCOTT, *My Paris.*
JUNE AKERS SEESE,
    Is This What Other Women Feel Too?
    What Waiting Really Means.
AURELIE SHEEHAN, *Jack Kerouac Is Pregnant.*
VIKTOR SHKLOVSKY, *Knight's Move.*
    A Sentimental Journey: Memoirs 1917-1922.
    Theory of Prose.
    Third Factory.
    Zoo, or Letters Not about Love.
JOSEF ŠKVORECKÝ,
    The Engineer of Human Souls.
CLAUDE SIMON, *The Invitation.*
GILBERT SORRENTINO, *Aberration of Starlight.*
    Blue Pastoral.
    Crystal Vision.
    Imaginative Qualities of Actual Things.
    Mulligan Stew.
    Pack of Lies.
    The Sky Changes.
    Something Said.
    Splendide-Hôtel.
    Steelwork.
    Under the Shadow.
W. M. SPACKMAN, *The Complete Fiction.*
GERTRUDE STEIN, *Lucy Church Amiably.*
    The Making of Americans.
    A Novel of Thank You.
PIOTR SZEWC, *Annihilation.*
STEFAN THEMERSON, *Tom Harris.*
JEAN-PHILIPPE TOUSSAINT, *Television.*
ESTHER TUSQUETS, *Stranded.*
DUBRAVKA UGRESIC, *Lend Me Your Character.*
    Thank You for Not Reading.
LUISA VALENZUELA, *He Who Searches.*
BORIS VIAN, *Heartsnatcher.*
PAUL WEST, *Words for a Deaf Daughter & Gala.*
CURTIS WHITE, *America's Magic Mountain.*
    The Idea of Home.
    Memories of My Father Watching TV.
    *Monstrous Possibility: An Invitation to Literary
        Politics.*
    Requiem.
DIANE WILLIAMS, *Excitability: Selected Stories.*
    Romancer Erector.
DOUGLAS WOOLF, *Wall to Wall.*
    Ya! & John-Juan.
PHILIP WYLIE, *Generation of Vipers.*
MARGUERITE YOUNG, *Angel in the Forest.*
    Miss MacIntosh, My Darling.
REYOUNG, *Unbabbling.*
LOUIS ZUKOFSKY, *Collected Fiction.*
SCOTT ZWIREN, *God Head.*

FOR A FULL LIST OF PUBLICATIONS, VISIT:
www.dalkeyarchive.com